FOREVER MAN
BOOK FIVE: BETRAYAL
CRAIG ZERF

Published by Anglo-American Press Limited

As always – to my wife, Polly and my son, Axel. You chase the shadows from my soul.

Once I said to a scarecrow, "You must be tired of standing in this lonely field."
And he said, "The joy of scaring is a deep and lasting one, and I never tire of it."
Said I, after a minute of thought, "It is true; for I too have known that joy."
Said he, "Only those who are stuffed with straw can know it."
Then I left him, not knowing whether he had complimented or belittled me.

Kahlil Gibran

Grim-son stood next to one of the myriad of camp fires and looked across the staging field. Over two hundred Vandals were scattered in groups around the fires. They had eaten earlier and now stood close to the flames, attempting to warm themselves up in the cold morning air. Some simply sat, quiet, introspected. Others played stones, a simple game that involved a board divided into quarters and six different colored stones. It was a child's game and the flyers played it because it allowed them to concentrate on something else beside the coming combat.

It had been over three months since the tribe of flying creatures had moved en masse behind the wall and thrown in their lot with the humans of the Free State of Scotland. Three months of almost constant fighting against the Annihilators—a race of insectoid beings that had followed the Vandals across the great divide and invaded the world of the humans. A warrior race that existed solely to prove their valor in battle.

Such was the threat provided by the Annihilators that the humans, led by Nathaniel Hogan, The Forever Man, were now forced into an uncomfortable alliance with their sworn enemies. They had formed a pact with the Fair-Folk and their minions, the Orcs, goblins, and trolls. An uneasy concord between two former enemies.

And, under the auspices of Tad and Roo, the Vandal leader, chief Cha-rek, had formed the Vandals into a well-ordered flying, fighting force. The whole thing had been based on similar structures to the British pre-pulse air force, complete with ranks and command structures.

Tad and Cha-rek had divided the Vandals into two major groups; fighters and ground attack. There were just over five thousand male Vandals of combat age. Of these, three thousand were designated as ground support and two thousand as fighters. The smaller, more nimble flyers were designated fighters and the larger Vandals, capable of carrying more weight, were designated as ground support.

The ground support carried a small, lightweight, double winged, or dual prod crossbow capable of firing two consecutive shots. As well as this, they carried six to eight pottery flasks filled with naphtha, a highly flammable distillation of peat, and super saturated sugar. The end result being a sticky, hard burning, homemade napalm bomb.

The top of each flask was stopped by a plug of linen and a rough flint and iron striker. So, all that the ground support Vandal would have to do is run his hand over the striker, thereby igniting the linen and then drop the flask onto the enemy, showering them in burning napalm. Of course, this had to be done whilst under attack by both archers and the enemy Yari, flying Annihilators, who would attempt to engage them in the air and rip them from the skies.

The fighters were equipped with a repeating crossbow based on the ancient Chinese *Ch-ko-nu* or continuous crossbow. A robust weapon with a ten-bolt magazine that could be primed and fired with one hand using a lever. After a little practice, it was possible to fire all ten bolts in under fifteen seconds and the weapon had a deadly range of around fifty yards. The fighters also carried a small casting net in a pouch on their belts. This was used to throw at another flying enemy and entangle them, forcing them to plunge to earth.

The fighters sole task was to protect the ground support Vandals so that they could deliver their burning payloads into the enemy ranks.

The Yari, or flying Annihilators, eschewed ranged weapons. They saw them as dishonorable and preferred to grapple hand-to-hand, using their natural bladed second set of appendages and their razor-clawed feet. Many of them were cut down by the nimble Vandal fighters before they came close enough to get to grips, taken out by either the repeating crossbows or the cast nets. But it was not easy. The Yari armored carapaces meant that they often had to be shot two or three times before they were out of the fight.

Because of this, the Vandals were getting the best of the aerial war, but they were severely outnumbered. In fact, Grim-son estimated that there were in excess of twenty thousand Yari. The enemy had a four-to-one advantage over the Vandal fighters.

Grim-son spotted Chief Cha-rek walking towards him, stopping every now and then to greet one of his Vandals. A quick word of encouragement, a grasp of the shoulder. Small things that made Cha-rek the beloved leader that he was.

He stopped in front of Grim-son.

'Wing Comm-ander,' he greeted.

'Chief,' answered Grim-son as he saluted in the Vandal fashion, both arms held out in front of his chest, palms facing up to show that he was unarmed.

'How are your figh-ters?'

‘Tired, Chief,’ said Grim-son. ‘But ready and keen as al-ways.’

‘Good. We expect an-other call soon. It seems as though the Annihilators have massed for an-other go at the wall. Not sure where. As usual they have con-centrated at three points, could be any of them. Or all,’ he added. ‘When the call comes I want you to take five hun-dred fighters up and cover eight hun-dred ground supp-ort. See how many of them you can burn out before they get to the wall. Make sure that you keep the Yari away from the ground supp-ort. Without those fire bombs the hu-mans will be over-run.’

Grim-son saluted and bowed, keeping his head down until the chief had gone on his way, spreading motivation and bolstering spirits wherever he went. The young Vandal wing commander took a deep breath. He hated this part of the day. Fear built up like a lead weight in your stomach, and the thought of dying became less of an abstract and more of a reality the more time spent thinking about it.

Grim-son knew that fear was like a barnacle build up on the hull of a ship, it built up below the water line where no one could see it, and then one day it sank you. Grim-son knew that most of his men were weighed down with fear at the moment and he wished that he could do more for them. As it was, all that he could do was show no fear and fly as hard and as fast as he could and kill as many Yari as possible.

Thirty minutes later they got the call and all fear disappeared in a rush of adrenalin. A female teenage human came running over. She was psychically connected to other teenagers on the wall, and when the Annihilators attacked, they would pulse a message. This message would be relayed to Grim-son and the Vandals would fly.

'Tower number two,' she shouted. 'Annihilators attacking in strength. Maybe six thousand, plus four thousand Yari.'

Grim-son wasted no time as he unfurled his leathern wings and jumped into the air, driving himself upwards with powerful beats. 'Scramble,' he shouted.

‘Ground support groups one to eight. Fighters, wings one to five. Form up on me, fighters we go high, ground support stay low, we’ll keep you covered.’

Within thirty minutes the Vandal group had formed up and were heading south for tower two on the wall.

Tad watched as the Annihilators started to march forward. Vast ranks of them neatly formed up in ten perfect squares of one thousand soldiers each. Their multicolored carapaces shone in the sun as they moved, a symphony of yellows and reds and greens. A veneer of festival like gaiety that covered a deep well of savage and brutal cruelty.

The Annihilators, or Roaches, as the humans had come to call them due to their insectoid-like appearance, were perfect warriors. Their top pair of limbs, attached to their shoulders like human arms, ended in natural blades some two-foot long, razor-sharp along one side and jaggedly serrated along the other.

Their second set of appendages protruded from the sides of their chest and they ended in three fingered graspers. Large, extremely powerful hands, capable of crushing a human throat or delivering a bludgeoning blow to the head or body. They used those same appendages for throwing spears and javelins and their range was quite phenomenal. Almost as far as a human archer could fire.

Their final appendages were legs, long and double-jointed bending backwards at the knee like horses' back legs and they provided the Roach with a powerful jump, kick and turn of speed.

But they were not innovative fighters. Their fighting style and swordsmanship was mired in basic patterns and set responses. Far removed from the human style

that verged on the random berserker method of fighting. Simply throwing everything that you had at the enemy until either you or they were vanquished.

Also—the humans were fighting for their families, for their king, for their country … and for their continued existence. Whereas the Roaches seemed to be fighting for little more than conquest. A way to prove themselves in the cauldron of battle. A test of their own courage and prowess. A ritual or a sacrament to combat as opposed to a battle for continued existence.

The Little Big Man walked along the battlement of the wall, and as he did, the warriors there all called to him. Shouting his name or simply giving him an 'Oorah.' There were swordsmen, spearmen with billhooks, archers, and axmen. Every fifty yards was a large catapult, next to it a pile of round boulders ready to fire at the advancing enemy.

He shouted back, laughing loudly, and making ribald comments. A man at ease before battle. And his demeanor lifted the spirits of all around him. For Tad was a dwarf in physical size only. His reputation, his leadership, and his skill in battle towered above his mere stature, for he was a man amongst men.

He stopped next to Bobby Tiernan, a teenage boy who had mere days ago turned sixteen, an age that allowed him to fight on the wall alongside the other men.

'Bobby,' he greeted.

The teenager saluted, fist to chest. He was dressed in a leather jerkin strengthened with squares of steel plate sewn in an overlapping pattern. Cotton trousers with hardened leather greaves, and leather forearm protectors. He was armed with a billhook, a short heavy spear with a hook at the bottom of the blade. The weapon

was perfect, both for punching through Roach carapaces and for hooking the tops of the Roach ladders and pulling them down.

'Little Big Man.'

Tad smiled. 'You ready?'

Bobby nodded. His face was pale, and Tad could see the thin sheen of cold sweat that coated his brow like a varnish. But his voice was steady.

'As ready as I will ever be, sir.'

Tad patted him on the shoulder. 'Good man.'

As he continued his walk, the Roaches started to move forwards, scraping their bladed forearms together as they did so. The noise was a high throbbing squeal. Like a giant child playing a broken violin. An awful disturbing dissonance that addled the brain and cramped the stomach.

Tad immediately climbed onto the crenulations on top of the wall and raised his voice in song. A powerful tenor that rang out over the insectoid screeching.

Mine eyes have seen the glory of the coming of the Lord;

He is trampling out the vintage where the grapes of wrath are stored;

He hath loosed the fateful lightning of His terrible swift sword:

His truth is marching on.

The rest of the men on the wall joined in for the chorus, shouting out the words in a lusty fashion, concerned more with volume than with pitch.

Glory, glory, hallelujah!
Glory, glory, hallelujah!
Glory, glory, hallelujah!
The truth is marching on.

And then the Little Big Man drew his sword, held it high above his head and then brought it chopping down. As one, the catapults on the wall opened up, lobbing their large boulders high into the sky, their crossbars cracking against the stops with a sound like thunder. Another gesture with the sword, and the archers drew and fired, filling the air with thousands of yard-long steel-tipped arrows.

Annihilator bodies were crushed under rocks and impaled by arrows as the storm of missiles marched across them. Then they were within javelin range and the Roaches started to retaliate, throwing their long, heavy pointed weapons that could cause serious injury if they struck home.

The humans ducked behind the

crenulations and waited for the javelin storm to rain down on them.

Then Tad heard a high-pitched whistling sound and his blood ran cold. He glanced up to see thousands of flying Yari above the wall. The whistling was the sound of the heavy steel darts that the Yari dropped from on high as they flew over.

An object travelling at a velocity of only two hundred feet per second is enough to penetrate the human skull. By the time the darts reached ground level they were travelling at over five hundred feet per second. This would impart sufficient energy to shatter shields, pierce armor, and literally punch straight through human flesh and bone.

'Take cover,' he shouted. 'Shields up.'

The defenders crouched down and pushed themselves up against the wall in an attempt to gain some semblance of protection from the falling missiles. Those who had shields held them over their heads, tilting them at an angle in the hope that the darts would ricochet off as they struck.

The steel storm struck with a sickening cacophony of sound. A rending of shields and armor, a tearing of flesh and a shattering of bone. The clamor of physical destruction was immediately swamped by the horrific sound of men screaming in agony.

And then, out of the sun, swooped the Vandals. In twenty-five wings of twenty each, the fighters plummeted through the air, wings folded tight as they swept down on the Yari.

The Vandals broke up the massive Yari formation as they barreled through them, and then as they pulled up, they unleashed their crossbow bolts. Hundreds of multicolored flying Roaches tumbled from the sky and the humans raised their voices in a loud cheer.

The ground support Vandals appeared over the tree tops, flying fast and low as they dropped their loads of homemade napalm on the advancing Annihilators and then jinked out of range of their archers as soon as they could.

A field of orange fire blossomed in the Roach ranks, followed by a cloud of black oily smoke.

But still they marched on, closing ranks, throwing more javelins as they approached. The ground support Vandals struck again and again, expending their bombs before they wheeled off and climbed high into the sky and headed for home.

Meanwhile, Grim-son and his fighters rolled and banked through the skies above, firing their crossbows and tangling Yari in their cast-nets.

Grim-son drove himself hard as he flew in behind a Yari that was about to grapple with one of the more

inexperienced Vandals, a youngster by the name of Rek-lee. The Yari flared his wings as he prepared to pounce. Grim-son lined up and fired. The bolt took the Yari in the back of the head and the creature spiraled down to earth in a flat spin, wings twitching spasmodically as it did so.

'Watch your back, boy,' he shouted at Rek-lee as he flew past, already looking for his next target.

All about him bodies spun and wheeled, diving and climbing. Others falling, broken winged. Plummeting to earth, flailing desperately as they struggled to stay alive, to keep airborne. To arrest their fatal plunge.

A bolt buzzed past Grim-son's ear. Friendly fire. Far too close for comfort. Out of his peripheral vision he saw a shadow bearing down on him, so he tucked in his left wing and rolled hard, dropping a hundred feet before he flared out and beat his wings hard, climbing back into the fray.

And then, like magic, the sky was clear. There were groups of Vandals, far distant, circling the wall. He cast his eyes around the sky but could see no sign of Yari although the ground was thickly littered with their broken, multicolored bodies.

During the dogfight he had flown

some four miles away from the wall, deep into enemy territory. He climbed high and pushed hard to get back above the enemy that were advancing on the wall, checking his crossbow magazine as he flew. Two bolts left. He had to be careful. His eyes flicked from side to side, scanning for enemy flyers. Nerves stretched as taut as a hangman's noose.

His final dash for home was without incident and as soon as he made it he checked on his men, reported the injuries and casualties to the executive officer, and then he curled up next to a fire, wrapped his wings around himself for added warmth, and immediately fell into an exhausted sleep.

The front rank of Annihilators threw their ladders against the wall and swarmed up, moving with incredible speed. Their numbers had been considerably thinned by the waves of napalm, and the catapults and archer fire. But there were still over six thousand of them in full fighting mettle.

Humans ran forward, and using billhooks, axes, spears, and bare hands, they pushed the ladders from the walls. Hundreds of Roaches fell as the ladders toppled, screeching and chittering as they did so.

But some of the Roaches made it to the top of the wall. It was here that Tad was needed most. Rallying troops and bolstering spirits. It was essential to prevent the Roaches from gaining a foothold on the battlements. He threw himself into the fray with dangerous abandon, swinging his battle axe and hacking into Roach legs and lower torsos, and then dispatching them when they fell to the ground.

Wherever Tad went, men followed. Desperate to fight alongside the Little Big Man. Eager to show him their commitment, their dedication, and their bravery. But also, they wanted to protect him. Because, as much as he was their leader, he was also their talisman.

A particularly large Roach made the top of the wall and cut down three defenders, creating a space for the next Annihilator to clamber up after him. Tad rushed to attack, knowing that, if they got another two or three warriors onto the wall, the humans would be hard-pressed to clear them off.

He jabbed his axe at the large Roach and then feinted left, dropped and rolled, springing up next to him and swinging hard, his blade slicing through the enemy's exoskeleton and severing his leg. Then he raised himself up onto one knee and swung again, bringing the axe down like he was chopping wood. The Roach's head leapt from his shoulders and bounced from the wall, hitting the ground below with a thud.

The Little Big Man wiped sweat from his forehead with the back of his hand, took a deep breath, and then bent down to retrieve his shield. As he did so, something struck him a glancing blow on the back of his head, knocking him to the floor. If he had not been leaning forward the blow would have hit him in the neck and his head would have joined the Roach's on the ground below.

As it was, he was in bad shape, his vision faded, and he struggled to get to his feet and turn to face the new threat. The Roach whipped one of its bladed arms down at him and Tad brought his shield up. But he knew that he was too late. His muscles were like jelly and his movements slow and uncoordinated. He braced for the strike.

It never came. Bobby jumped in front of the Roach, swinging his billhook as he did so, shouting his defiance. The

Annihilator brushed aside the teenager's attack with contemptuous ease, grabbing his billhook with one of his appendages, and then striking down with another. The blow struck Bobby above his right elbow, severing his arm with one clean cut. The Roach followed up with another strike, slashing deep into Bobby's torso, ripping through his leather armor, and slicing through muscle and ribs.

Bobby grunted and fell to his knees, desperately clutching at his wound as he did so.

Behind the Roach, more Annihilators made the top of the ladder and clambered onto the wall, forming a fighting wedge.

Tad screamed his anguish and attacked, spinning like a dervish as he did so, his axe a blur of bloodied steel. The Roaches slashed and cut back at him, but he moved too fast, his body powered by wrath and a need for vengeance.

His frenzied attack galvanized the human defenders, and with a mighty effort, they cleared the rest of the ladders from the wall, and the archers drove the waves of Annihilators back.

Tad rushed over to Bobby, knelt next to him, and took his head in his hands.

‘Hey, Little Big Man,’ Bobby whispered.

‘Hey, Bobby.’

‘I’m hurt bad,’ said the teenager.

‘Not so bad,’ lied Tad. ‘Just rest. We’ll get Gogo to take a look at you. Sort you out. Have you back on the wall in no time at all.’

Bobby smiled. ‘I think that you’re right. I can’t feel any pain. That’s a good thing, isn’t it?’ he asked.

‘Yeah. That’s a good thing.’

‘I must have been knocked out for some time,’ murmured Bobby.

‘What do you mean?’ asked Tad.

‘Been out for a while,’ continued Bobby. ‘It must be the middle of the night. Can’t even see anything.’

A tear slid down Tad’s cheek, but he

kept his voice strong. Confident. ‘Yeah. It’s dark, Bobby. Don’t worry about it. Rest.’

Bobby took a deep shuddering breath and then his body went limp.

Tad held him for a while more and then lay his head gently down, stood up, and readied the men for the next attack.

The Forever Man, Marine Master Sergeant Nathaniel Hogan, King of the Free State, leader of the Picts, and Protector of Humanity, turned to Orc Sergeant Kob and spoke.

'I miss ice cream,' he said. 'Chocolate chip.'

Kob stared at The Forever Man for a while before he answered. As per usual, the Orc understood most of the individual words that Nathaniel had uttered, but he had no idea what The Forever Man was actually talking about.

Finally, he said something. 'What is ice cream?'

'It's basically frozen cream.'

Kob nodded. 'I have seen cream freeze. In the winter. What is chocolate?'

Nathaniel thought for a bit. 'Not sure,' he admitted. 'It's sweet. Lots of sugar. And cocoa beans. I think.'

'What is a cocoa bean?'

Nathaniel shrugged. 'It's brown.'

'I see,' said Kob. 'Brown, frozen cream. Sounds delicious … anything else that you miss?'

'Whatever,' said the Marine. 'I suppose that you had to be there at the time.' He raised a pair of binoculars to his eyes and gazed across the valley. 'They're walking right into the trap,' he said. 'Is everyone ready?' enquired Nathaniel, referring to the mix of Orcs and goblins and humans that made up the allied squad. 'Another ten minutes and we can spring our surprise.'

Kob grunted his approval and then whispered a command to the Orc next to him. The Orc crept off to spread the word amongst the rest of the allied warriors that lined the narrow valley, waiting in ambush as they had been for over eight hours now.

Nathaniel had left Tad, Roo, and Papa

Dante in charge of the wall, trusting them to repel any Annihilator attacks.

While they did that, he had put together a commando group that worked behind enemy lines. A group of one hundred elite troops. A mixture of humans, Orcs, and goblins. He had not included Vandals as, even though he would have loved some air support, any flying would certainly give away their position, and stealth was their primary goal.

They struck hard and they struck fast. Cutting enemy supply lines, wiping out patrols, and laying false tracks to feed the Roaches bogus information. They were a constant thorn in the enemy's side.

Eight hours previously, as the sun rose, twenty of Nathaniel's commandos had fired at a column of Roaches, causing several casualties. Then they had run, leaving a faint but discernable track.

The enemy had pursued them, but the commandos had avoided capture whilst still remaining in enemy range for most of the day. Now, a few hours before sunset, they were leading the group of six hundred Annihilators into a well laid ambush.

The commando group consisted of fifty goblin archers, thirty Orcs, and twenty humans. Twenty of the goblins had been used to bait the trap. The other thirty lined the narrow valley in defilade, concealed behind rocks and fallen trees.

The Orcs had been placed at a pinch point in the valley, dug in and covered with brush and heather, invisible even from as close as ten yards. Then Nathaniel had placed the humans in the forest close to the side of the ambush, ready to run down and cut off any escape once the trap had been sprung, encircling the Roaches completely.

It was a solid plan. A good plan.

It was also a very dangerous plan, because even after the goblin archers had thinned out the Roach ranks, the commandos would be outnumbered at least seven or eight to one.

But then, none of the enemy was—The Forever Man.

The retreating goblins passed the

entrance to the ambush and immediately split into two groups, scuttling under cover to join their comrades.

As they reached them, Nathaniel conjured up a fireball and launched it straight up into the air like a flare.

That was the signal to spring the trap.

As one, the goblins opened up, firing fast and with deadly accuracy.

Nathaniel did not like the goblins. He found them to be obtuse, surly, and untrustworthy. But he had no trouble admitting that they were superb bowmen. Their over-long arms and massively developed shoulders ensured that they could easily draw their six-foot longbows and fire up to ten arrows a minute. The bows were rated at over one hundred and fifty pounds pull-weight, and the arrow, when fired, was capable of penetrating even the thickest armor.

Thirty Roaches went down under the arrow storm before they had even realized that they were under attack.

Nathaniel waited until the

Annihilators recovered from the initial shock and started to reform, closing their ranks as they prepared to charge up the hill at the archers. Then he raised his axe in the air and brought it chopping down. That was the signal for the Orcs to break out from their concealment and charge the enemy.

Shouting their traditional war cry as they ran, the Orcs broke cover and sprinted at the Roaches, broadswords raised as they did so.

'*Kamateh,*' they shouted. '*Kamateh!* Kill, kill them all.'

The fighting wedge of the Orcs crashed into the ranks of Roaches, slashing and cutting as they did so. The Annihilators reeled under the onslaught as they struggled to fight on three sides.

Then Nathaniel threw another fireball into the sky.

The humans ran out from their cover and charged, smashing into the unsuspecting rear of the Roach formation.

The Marine drew in a little power and

used it to enhance his voice, speaking directly to the goblin archers.

'Advance,' he said. 'Get in close. Don't let them rally.'

The goblins walked slowly down the hill on each side of the mêlée, firing arrows as they did.

Nathaniel and Kob watched the battle closely as it progressed. It was going well. The Roaches had been taken completely by surprise and were reeling under the unsuspected onslaught.

However, they were a well-disciplined, battle hardened group and it was only a matter of time before they started to rally and then their superior numbers would start to tell.

The Forever Man waited another full minute before he turned to Kob with a grin.

'Right, my friend,' he said. 'It's time that you and I entered the fray. Let's finish this.'

Kob nodded. Unlike Nathaniel, he did not smile. It takes twelve different sets of muscles to smile and the Orcs were possessed of none of them. But he did bare his fangs in a facsimile of the expression and that was good enough for Nathaniel.

The Marine slapped the Orc on the shoulder.

'Let's go.'

'*Kamateh!*' yelled Kob.

The two warriors sprinted down the hill and joined the battle.

Kob fought using a buckler and a broadsword. The small shield was perfect for both protection and attack and the Orc would wield it like a weapon, smashing into his opponents, pushing them off balance and then dispatching them with his massive sword. It was a combat style that combined controlled aggression with power and weight, as opposed to speed and dexterity.

Nathaniel was a different story. He fought in a fashion that was completely unique. He paid no attention whatsoever to defense. All about attack, he relied solely on his superhuman, gamma-ray-enhanced speed. His double-bladed axe spun and flickered through the air at speeds so fast as to defy the eye. Like death on gossamer wings, it danced a graceful ballet. Dipping and rising and slashing and cutting. A silver crescent of light that brought a violent end to all that it came in contact with.

Such was the effect of these two great warriors it was as if another whole battalion had suddenly entered the fray. The Annihilators screeched and spat as they were driven back by the great Orc and the axe-wielding Forever Man. And though the Roach discipline was as strong as steel, even steel has its breaking point. Chains can be pulled apart, sword blades shattered, and plate armor riven in twain. It is simply a matter of how much pressure is applied.

The goblins were now less than fifty yards away and were firing point-blank into the massed Roaches. The Orcs were smashing deep into the enemy's ranks, compacting them together as they surged forward.

Kob and Nathaniel's charge was the

final weight that tilted the axis of the battle.

The Annihilators turned and ran. Only to come up against the human warriors who had formed a shield wall. Large wood and steel shields interlocked tight as they charged forward to check the Roach retreat dead in its tracks.

The rest of the battle was a simple exercise in extermination.

Blood flowed like water and the shrill shrieks of dying Roaches filled the air.

By the time the sun went down, not one living Annihilator was left on the field. Nathaniel had seen a few escape, slipping away in the heat of the battle, but he wasn't that worried. He would let them go as it wasn't worth the risk involved to track them down.

Happy with the day's work, he instructed his warriors to look to their wounded prior to heading for home.

Akimiri Hijiti, the undisputed Hatomoto, or Supreme Warrior of the Annihilators, stood on his ceremonial plinth, flanked by his three Busho, High Warriors and the chief Yari. In front of him a rank of seven Chugan, Standard Warriors, lay prostrate on the ground, their faces pressed into the dirt.

The seven Chugan had arrived mere moments earlier. They were the only survivors of an ambush that had taken place the day before. They had escaped from the clutches of the enemy and had run back to base camp in order to tell the Hatomoto the news.

They told the story with no embellishment or falsities, neither exaggerating nor playing down what had happened.

Supreme Commander Hijit ensured that he had complete control of his feelings before he reacted to the Chugan's story. To show a surfeit of emotion would be unacceptable and would result in serious loss of face.

'So,' he said. 'You are telling me that a mere handful of the enemy managed to defeat an entire Grist of eight hundred warriors?'

'I affirm,' answered one of the prostrate Chugan.

'How?'

'Their tactics were masterful,' continued the Chugan. 'As well as this, they were led by the Lightning Warrior.'

Hijiti took a deep breath. Now it made more sense. The Lightning Warrior, or Forever Man as he was also called, was a warrior of note. Many reports had come back to the commander about the Lightning Warrior's prowess in battle and it was quite possible that this single man could turn the outcome of a battle. He knew because it was something that he had done many times over.

'Is there anything else that you need to tell me?'

'Yes, Supreme Commander,' barked the Chugan. 'At the Lightning Warrior's side was the Outstanding One. With the two of them fighting together we were unable to prevail.'

The Outstanding one. The Orc that was unlike an Orc. The one who stood out from all of the other almost identical ones. Bigger, faster, better. Oh, how the Supreme Commander wanted to meet either of these warriors in single combat. The honor would be immense. The pleasure in beating them, incomparable. In fact, even a loss against such outstanding warriors would be honorable.

'Supreme Commander,' continued the Chugan. 'May we ask a boon of you?'

'Speak,' commanded Hijiti.

'We have dishonored ourselves by leaving the field of battle,' said the Chugan. 'But we felt that you might need the information that we had, regarding the

Lightning Warrior and the Outstanding One. However, we now beg your permission to commit ourselves to the blade. Please allow us the rite of *Johgaki.'*

Hijiti nodded. 'Let it be so,' he said as he beckoned to one of his Busho. 'Ikara, do the honors.'

The Busho High Warrior called Ikara approached the prostrate Chugans and commanded them to raise themselves to their knees. Once the Chugans were all kneeling, Ikara walked to the side of the parade area and scouted about for a while. Eventually he found a patch of small white Daisies. He carefully cut seven of them and then lay one in front of each of the Chugan warriors.

The flowers represented innocence, virtue, and blamelessness. As opposed to guilt.

He stood above the first Chugan.

'Reach for the flower,' he instructed. 'And there you will find your purity.'

'In purity I shall be reborn,' said the Chugan as he lent forward to touch the flower.

As his hand touched the bloom Ikara brought his bladed forearm down, severing the Chugan's head from his torso. The rite of *Johgaki* had been successful and the Chugan's spirit was free to enter the realm of his ancestors without shame.

Ikara took a step forward and instructed the next Chugan to reach for the flower.

The rite took place seven times and then the bodies were taken away for ritual burning.

'We need to talk,' said Hijiti when the bodies had been cleared away.

The Bushos and the chief Yari gathered around the Supreme Commander and waited for him to speak.

'These humans are proving more difficult to overcome than I first thought,' he said. 'When we first came across them I thought them to be weak and undisciplined. We destroyed their villages and their people at will and whim with little opportunity to do proper battle.

However, it appears that they do have a warrior class after all. This is good as I feared that we would have no chance to gain honor through combat. Now, however, I start to fear the opposite. We have yet to have one decisive victory against the human warrior classes. All that we have achieved thus far is the subjugation of their farmers and peasant classes. They have defeated us at the wall and their strikes against our camps and patrols have resulted in numerous losses for us.

Although it is true that honor is found in battle, it is hard to find honor in constant loss. I give my permission for you to speak. Why are we not winning?'

'With all respect, Supreme Commander,' voiced Ikara. 'We are not losing.'

'Granted,' admitted Hijiti. 'But the lack of losing does not equate to winning.'

'We are having more success against the gray people and their Orcs and goblins,' said the chief Yari. 'In fact, we have won two or three major battles against them.'

'No, we have not,' countered Hijiti. 'We have simply caused them to retreat, and they have done so in good order and without major loss of life. Actually, it seems to me as if the gray people are avoiding any major confrontation even though there are a substantial number of them. I would say that they outnumber the humans by a factor of five or six to one.'

'That is true,' agreed the chief Yari. Their Orcs and goblins are adequate warriors and they are very numerous, but they are definitely holding back. Perhaps they are waiting to launch a major offensive.'

'Keep a close eye on them,' commanded Hijiti. 'And in the meanwhile, we must redouble our efforts against the humans. Step up the number of patrols and we shall put together another attack on the wall. We shall also look for other areas of combat. It is time to bring these humans to heel.'

The Bushos and the chief Yari bowed deeply and left, walking backwards for the first twenty yards to show their respect.

And Hatomoto, Akimiri Hijiti, Supreme Warrior of the Annihilators, stood alone and thought about fighting the Lightning Warrior.

The Unicorn had visited The Forever Man in his dreams the night before. He had given both advice and instruction. Neither had made much sense.

But Nathaniel had already accepted the fact that the Unicorn was a being that had access to otherworldly information that he was not akin to, and as such, his advice did not necessarily have to make sense—it merely had to be believed.

So, he had called Papa Dante in order to give him a task.

Nathaniel had not seen Papa for a while and he greeted the leader of the walking folk with a welcoming smile.

Papa Dante tried to smile back but the expression came out as a grimace instead.

'You're in pain,' noted Nathaniel as

he placed his hand on his friend's shoulder.

'It is nothing,' said Papa Dante. 'A mug of Gogo's brandy and it will recede.'

'What is it?' asked Nathaniel with a grin. 'Your old body can't take the pace anymore?'

'I wish,' said Papa. 'According to Gogo it is the cancer. Liver. Always thought that the drink would get me. Or smoking. Not some ugly little tumor, sneaking up like a thief in the night and stealing me away.'

Nathaniel went pale as the import of what Papa Dante was saying hit him. 'I had no idea. When did you find out? Can Gogo do something about it?'

Papa shook his head. 'Known for a couple of days. Thought that it was just bad backache. Went to see Gogo. There's naught that she can do. Brandy and herbs for the pain. Different herbs if I want to take a quicker way out at a later stage.'

'My God,' whispered Nathaniel. 'How long?'

Papa shrugged. 'Enough time left to plant a vegetable garden and reap the rewards, but not enough time to plant a tree and ever sit in its shade.'

'Months?'

'Yes. But not years.'

'I am sorry,' said Nathaniel.

'Not your fault,' quipped Papa Dante. 'God's will.'

Nathaniel sat silent for a while. Papa had always been one of his dearest friends and some part of Nathaniel thought that he would always be there. Not immortal, but somehow, everlasting. He was also one of the Marine's most trusted advisors but there was no way that he could task Papa with a job now. Not when he only had months left to live.

'Well then,' said Papa. 'What did you call me here for? Out with it.'

Nathaniel shook his head. 'It was nothing,' he said. 'It can wait. No rush.'

Papa leaned forward. 'Listen, my friend,' he said. His voice low. Earnest.

'Talk to me. Do not make me spend the last months of my life feeling useless. Fading away like an old photo. A mere facsimile of what I once was. I'm not dead yet.'

The Marine nodded. 'Okay, Papa,' he said. 'I get it.'

'Good. Now, let's try again. What did you call me here for?'

Nathaniel nodded. 'Okay, if you say so. We need to rebuild the Antonine Wall.'

'The Antonine Wall,' repeated Papa Dante. 'So, what is the Antonine Wall when it's at home?'

'The Romans built it,' answered Nathaniel. 'Around 142 AD. Runs from the Firth of Forth to the Firth of Clyde. Originally an earth rampart and a ditch nine feet high and fifteen feet wide. I need it rebuilt in stone and brick if possible. Tear down any and all buildings in the area to furnish materials, this is important. Ten-foot high with watchtowers, the whole deal. That's about thirty-nine miles long. And I need it done fast.'

‘If I am to see its end then I also need it to be done with haste,’ agreed Papa Dante. ‘May I ask why?’

‘Because it needs to be done,’ answered Nathaniel.

‘If it needs to be turned around with some haste then I shall need a lot of men. Maybe as many as ten thousand. Maybe more. And this at a time when we need all of the able-bodied men that we can to man the existing wall. People will want to know why?’

‘Why?’ asked Nathaniel. ‘Because I am their king. Because I am The Forever Man. Because I say so.’

‘That’s good enough for me,’ said Papa.

‘And it shall be good enough for the people,’ retorted The Forever Man. ‘I want Roo to go with you. Start as soon as possible. Take all of the men that you need. Check with Tad. Also, try to use as many women as you can. They are just as capable, and many of them are as strong.’

Papa nodded and stood up, wincing

slightly as he did so. 'Thank you, Nathaniel,' he said. 'I will not let you down. You have given my last moments a purpose. I am in your debt.'

Nathaniel smiled. 'You shall never be in my debt, friend,' he said. 'Never.'

Papa left, and The Forever Man sat alone with his thoughts.

Tad arched his back in an attempt to stretch the kinks out. He and twenty of his men had been in the saddle for over a week now on an extended patrol into Annihilator territory. Unlike the mixed crew of humans, Orcs, and goblins that he was used to working with, this patrol consisted only of heavily armed humans. They were all on horseback.

Usually, horses were out of the question, because try as they might, they had been unable to train any horse to accept an Orc on its back. The animals simply went wild when an Orc approached them. Goblins were fine. Accepted by the horses but not loved. The goblins feelings were mutual.

Tad was much happier with a solely human contingent. He still didn’t trust the

Fair-Folk minions even though they were, technically, allies. He felt that they did not give their all in battle. Particularly the goblins that seemed only to do the bare minimum to stay out of trouble. And both they, and the Orcs, never took advantage of a tactical situation. They would fight until the enemy was on the back foot and then they would often simply stop, letting the humans finish the encounter.

None of the actual Fair-Folk, or 'rubber heads' as the humans were now calling them, ever deigned to be on the actual field of battle. Fair-Folk's new derisory nickname had come about ever since their true forms had been revealed in the last battle before the Annihilators came. And the closest that any rubber head would come to being involved, was to sit on the very peripheries of a set battle and then only in an advisory capacity.

Tad had spoken to Nathaniel about it on numerous occasions, but the Marine had simply nodded and told Tad to do his best. The Little Big Man was frustrated, but aside from being his friend, the Marine was also his king, so he did not argue. He simply did as he was told. He did his best.

He was pulled out of his reverie by a smell. The smell of smoke on the wind. Strong and acrid. He had smelled it before. It was more than mere wood-fire smoke. This was the smell of a household burning. The smell of thatch, wood, cotton, mattresses, and livestock going up in flames. It was the smell of war.

Tad turned in his saddle and spoke to the man riding next to him. 'Jackson, ride ahead, see where that smoke is coming from and get back as soon as.'

Jackson saluted and spurred his horse into a gallop, moving towards the column of smoke that was now clearly visible rising above the surrounding tree tops.

Two minutes later Jackson came galloping back.

'Roaches,' he shouted. 'Attacking a homestead. Women and children. Follow me.'

'Let's ride,' yelled Tad and they thundered after Jackson, weaving through the trees at top speed.

As one, they burst into an open area. A grazing paddock set next to a burning farmhouse. Three bodies lay in front of the house. All male. All dead, slashed and broken.

A young woman stood in the clearing, broadsword in her hand. Behind her, two young girls, perhaps seven and ten years old.

And, in front of the woman were nine Annihilators, walking slowly towards her.

Without pause, Tad drew his axe and charged into the Roaches, hacking and cutting as he did so. He fought like a man possessed, his axe flying from side to side as he wheeled his mount, striking both left and right with mighty overhand blows. The Roach warriors tried to fight back but Tad was simply moving too fast and too aggressively.

Before his men could help, the Little Big Man had laid out all nine Annihilators. He reined his horse in, jumped off and moved quickly from body to body, hacking off their heads with his axe. Ensuring their deaths.

Finally, he stopped and drew breath. Panting fast and deep like a caged animal. He felt a hand on his shoulder and he spun and raised his axe.

'It's only me,' said the woman.

'Sorry,' said Tad. 'I meant no harm.'

The woman lent forward and kissed Tad on the cheek, her long blond hair brushed against his face as she did. It smelled of apples and felt like spun silk. 'Thank you,' she said.

'Apples,' said Tad.

She raised a quizzical eyebrow. 'I'm sorry. What?'

'Your hair,' answered Tad. 'It smells of apples. And silk. Well, it doesn't smell of silk. I don't know what silk smells like. I …' Tad paused. 'I'm sorry. I'm normally less idiotic than this. I apologize. My name is Tad.' He held out his hand.

She took it and squeezed. 'I am Maryanne. I have heard of you,' she continued. ‘The Little Big Man. Leader of the Free State army and advisor to the king.’

‘Yes,’ said Tad. ‘That would be me.’

The two little girls ran over and put their arms around Maryanne.

‘This is Stephanie, and this is Clare,’ introduced Maryanne. ‘My daughters.’

Tad struggled to keep the disappointment from showing on his face. ‘Oh. Daughters. Pleased to meet you,’ he said to the girls as he bowed. ‘I am sorry that we did not arrive sooner … your father?’ Tad gestured towards the bodies.

‘He died some years ago,’ said Maryanne.

‘Oh, good,’ said Tad and then he blushed bright red. ‘I am so sorry. I didn’t mean that. I cannot apologize enough. I simply mean that I am glad that he did not die now. It appears that your beauty has rendered me into an idiot,’ he continued. ‘Please allow my men and me to help you, my lady. We are at your service.’

It didn't take long to ascertain that it would no longer be possible for Maryanne and her daughters to stay at the farm. The house had been burned to the ground and the farmhands and livestock killed. As well as that, the area was remote, in Annihilator controlled territory, and would surely come up against Roach attacks again as it seemed that the Roaches had decided to step up their campaign of late.

The family had lost all of their possessions in the fire, so Tad repacked four of the packhorses, redistributing the soldier's loads to free up two of the horses. Then he threw a saddle blanket over the horses and the two girls rode one and Maryanne the other.

They were all well practiced horse riders and rode with grace and ease, so after Tad had seen this, he pushed them hard, hoping to make home before nightfall or at least shortly afterwards.

Commander Ammon Set-Bat of the Fair-Folk shook his head in disgust and he turned to Seth Hil-Nu, his chief mage.

'Have you read this?' he asked.

Seth shook his head. 'It has only just arrived via horse courier. It came straight to you.'

'It is a missive from the human king. The so-called Forever Man. It is a formal complaint regarding the state of our troops and their deportment in battle. He claims that they are holding back.'

Seth paused for a while before he spoke. 'Well, they are.'

'I know that,' agreed Ammon. 'But it insults us to say that they are.'

'The thing is, Commander,' replied

Seth. 'We have told them to do the bare minimum. Avoid confrontation if possible. Allow the humans to take the lead in any charges, put survival above winning. Basically, ensure that the humans are drained at a rate that exceeds ours. And we knew that, after a time, it would start to become obvious.'

'I know all of that, Seth,' grunted Ammon. 'They were my orders and I am not grotesquely stupid.'

Seth bowed deeply. 'Forgive me, Commander. I was stating the obvious. I beg forgiveness.'

'I wonder,' continued Ammon. 'If, perhaps we could take this whole idea a little further.'

'In what way, Commander?'

'I'm not sure. What do you think would happen if we simply pulled out of the alliance? Fortify a line across the country, through London. A series of fortified emplacements from Severn Beach to Gravesend.'

'Initial thoughts,' said Seth. 'The

Annihilators will most probably mass up and attack us. Without a formal arrangement they would simply assume that we were retreating or consolidating for an assault of some sort. Might bring on more aggressive attention than we want.'

'I shall think about it,' said Commander Ammon. 'I am sure that there is something that we can do. The mere thought of being allied to the humans makes me feel ill.'

'Likewise, Commander,' agreed Seth. 'Likewise.'

Captain Axel Judge, leader of the abbey and formerly of the Queen's Royal Surrey Regiment, handed the rider a sealed letter. 'Donavan, take this and ride as fast as you can to the Fair-Folk encampment in the Hope Valley. Give this to the rubber head in command and tell him that we need reinforcements ASAP. A large force of Roaches is approaching from the north. We will hold as long as possible. Ride hard and bring them back. We are relying on you, Donavan. Now go.'

The rider spurred his horse and galloped off through the abbey gates. The gates closed behind him with a rattle of chain and a grinding of pulleys.

One of the long-range scouts had reported in that morning with news that a massive contingent of Annihilators were marching on the abbey. Axel had immediately rung the alarm bells, and with well-rehearsed speed and efficiency, the surrounding farmers and traders had converged on the abbey, bringing supplies, weapons, and family to both shelter behind and protect the abbey walls.

Then he had split the combat able men and women into three equal groups. Each group would spend eight hours on the walls so that they would not be taken by surprise. There were large stocks of arrows, throwing spears, and pots of oil placed along the wall, ready to bombard the Roaches as soon as they came in range.

Axel had also placed his entire cavalry; some two hundred well armored and heavily armed men, outside the abbey. They were well hidden in the woods to the south west of the abbey and were there to bolster the Fair-Folk when they arrived, providing cavalry to an army that had none due to the fact that the horses could not abide Orcs.

Now, with Donavan on his way to fetch reinforcements from the Fair-Folk, there was nothing to do except wait.

Axel walked back to his study, popping into the small chapel before he did to invite Father O'Hara for a drink and a chat, an invitation that the old Irish priest accepted with alacrity.

'So,' said the father as they walked to Axel's study. 'You have sent for de rubber heads for reinforcements. Do you tink dat dey will come?'

Axel nodded. 'They'll come, Father. I just hope that they get here in time. We can hold for a day at most, but the scouts tell of nigh on ten thousand Roaches coming our way. We've beaten off small attacks before, as you know, two or three thousand. But this is a very different kettle of fish. It's obvious that they mean to exterminate us this time.'

They entered the study and Axel went to the cupboard and took out a bottle of brandy and two balloon snifters.

An unopened bottle of genuine pre-pulse, Remy Martin VSOP.

Father O'Hara raised an eyebrow.

‘Axel, you does know, boyo, dat is most likely de only bottle of Remy Martin left in de entire world?’

Axel nodded as he cracked the seal and poured two very generous measures of the dark golden spirit. The honey and leather smell saturated the room, bringing back memories of a time before. Memories of electric lighting and central heating. Music systems, 24-hour television, and instant coffee.

A time when boys of sixteen were scholars, as opposed to axe-wielding warriors on the wall. Where danger meant forgetting to put on enough sunscreen, or jaywalking. Not charging an enemy formation or standing under an arrow storm.

Axel raised his glass. ‘To the past,’ he toasted.

But Father O’Hara shook his head. ‘No, my friend. To the present, for that is all that we have left.’

They clinked crystal and drank.

‘I’m only glad that the Prof is no

longer here to see all of this. He hated war and violence. Especially near the end,' said Axel, talking about the professor who used to be the leader of the abbey when it was still a school, and before Axel took over. Before the pulse. Before the madness.

The door opened and Janice, Axel's wife, walked in. She took one look at the open bottle of Remy Martin and her eyes teared up. She walked over to Axel and put her arms around him. They didn't speak, merely held each other. Eventually, Axel gently pulled away.

'I must see to the defenses,' he said.

Janice nodded. Kissed him once, gently.

'I tink dat I might sample a little more of dis fine spirit,' said Father O'Hara. 'Den I shall take myself to da chapel and put in a bit of prayer time. Ask da almighty for a hand.'

Axel nodded. 'Do so, Father. We need all the help that we can get.' Then he faced Janice. 'The Fair-Folk will come,' he said. 'All we have to do is hold the Roaches until then.'

He left the study, picking up his broadsword as he did.

Then he crossed the quad and climbed the stairs to the battlements above the gate. His people called out to him as he stood on the walkway, their shouts of 'Captain,' ringing out across the square.

He replied with a salute and a smile. 'Are you ready?' he shouted.

A cheer of affirmation thundered out as all shouted their approbation. As the cheering faded another sound could be heard in the background. Like the wind rushing across the plains. A rhythmic rustling susurration of sound.

It was the sound of over ten thousand pairs of legs brushing through the long grass in the fields that surrounded the abbey. It was the sound of approaching death.

As was the Annihilator custom, they arrayed themselves opposite the gates in neat ranks of one thousand. Ten ranks. Above them, skittering across the sky, were at least another thousand of the flying Yari.

Captain Axel had command of almost three thousand armed men and women on his walls. Enough to hold them. For a while at least.

He knew exactly how the attack would take place. The Annihilators were nothing if not predictable. They would wait until their ranks had settled and then, as one they would move forward, the front ranks holding ladders at the ready. Then, as soon as they were in range, the spears would be unleashed. At the same time the Yari would drop their darts from on high in a storm of death-delivering steel.

The ladders would be thrown up against the wall and the battle would commence. The same procedure would be repeated until one or the other side came out on top.

It was almost prosaic. Apart from all the blood and screaming and dying.

The Roaches charged. The humans waited, shields at the ready. Five thousand spears filled the sky and crashed down on the wall, punching the defenders back, killing and maiming. A thousand steel darts rained down from on high, sundering shields and splitting skulls.

Axel stood up and raised his sword. 'Archers. Fire.'

Two thousand cloth-yard shafts arched through the air, followed by another two thousand and another. A slithering bridge of death. Droves of Roaches were driven to the floor as six thousand hardwood shafts struck home.

And then the front rank hit the wall. Ladders were raised, and the Roaches swarmed up.

'Oil!' shouted Axel.

Men scurried forward and emptied pots of fish oil over the sides of the walls. Hundreds of gallons.

'Flame!' commanded the captain.

Burning torches were cast over the side and the humans pulled hastily back.

The oil took flame with a dull

explosion. The sound of a giant dog barking once. Flames leapt a hundred feet into the air.

Ladders and Annihilators burned alike as the smoky orange fire consumed them.

The Roaches withdrew to the plain to reform. Once again in neat ranks of one thousand.

But this time there were only nine ranks. Not ten.

Axel walked the wall, talking to his warriors. Young, old, men, and women. His people.

The Annihilators struck again one more time before nightfall. But this time, the humans had no more oil, and many groups of Roaches made the top of the walls and were only dispatched after much desperate hand-to-hand combat.

Finally, they were driven back.

But after that assault, laid out in neat rows on the quad, were over four hundred human bodies.

Axel prayed fervently that the Fair-

Folk reinforcements would come the next day. He did not sleep that night, rather spending his time talking to the wounded, bolstering spirits, and sitting with his wife Janice.

The Annihilators attacked again at sunrise.

Again, at midday.

And again, three hours before sunset.

By the time the sun went down on the second day, there was no longer any space in the quad for the bodies of the fallen, and Captain Axel had ordered them to be laid out in the gardens behind the chapel.

Over one thousand souls had departed over the last twenty-four hours.

Father O'Hara, like Axel, had not yet slept as he gave last rites to the dying, said prayers over the dead, and provided succor for the wounded.

The Fair-Folk reinforcements had not come. Neither had Donavan returned with news, although even if he had wanted to, Axel knew of no way that he could have made it through enemy lines and into the abbey.

The next dawn brought yet more death, the morning light shining on the fields of blood and the enemy carapaces and the weary faces of the defenders alike.

As the Annihilators started their next attack a sound of thunder shook the ground as hundreds of mounted men came galloping out of the forest to strike at the enemy flank. They drove deeply into the Roach formations, cutting and trampling as they charged.

A cheer went up amongst the defenders.

'The Fair-Folk have come!'

'The reinforcements are here!'

But their joy was short-lived as it became obvious that there were no reinforcements. No Orc warriors. No goblin archers.

It was merely the desperate charge of the human cavalry that had been kept in reserve.

At their head rode Donovan, the young scout who had ridden out to bring the Fair-Folk reinforcements. He had returned alone.

The cavalry fought bravely, hacking and chopping as they went down under the thousands of Annihilator warriors.

And then there were none.

The defenders looked on in utter silence, faces set. Expressions resolute. A people that had accepted their fate.

Miraculously they lasted another three days.

Three days of almost constant battle.

When the gates were finally breached, and the Annihilators burst into the abbey, there were but twenty-six humans left alive.

And at their head stood the bleeding, broken figure of Captain Axel Judge, formally of the Queen's Royal Surrey Regiment and leader of the abbey.

Behind him arrayed a selection of men, women, and children. All were armed. At his feet lay the body of his beloved wife.

And the captain remembered.

He remembered his friends, Patrick and Dom, and his sister Jenny. His family home in the village of Judge's Cross. How he had battled against the Belmarsh boys, a gang of thugs and murderers, rapists, and thieves. How he had lost both the battle and his right eye and almost his life. How this had led him to meet the absolute love of his life, Janice, who had saved him and then later taken him as her husband.

Most of all he remembered The Forever Man. If only he were here now. He knew, without shadow of doubt, that the Marine would be able to, somehow, turn the tide.

But, as his father used to always say, if wishes were horses then beggars would eat horse meat.

And Axel held his sword above his head and smiled one last time as he charged at the enemy that had destroyed his people.

Tad laughed and picked up Clare and put her on his shoulders. Although the ten-year-old was only slightly shorter than the Little Big Man he carried her like she wasn't even there such was his amazing strength.

Then he picked up Stephanie in the crook of his arm and ran, jumping over logs and tufts of grass, neighing like a horse as he did so.

Both of the girls squealed with delight and Maryanne joined in with his laughter.

Finally, Tad put the girls down and walked over to Maryanne. His breathing was even and there was no hint that he had been exerting himself.

Maryanne smiled at him as he came to her. Even now, after only ten days, she knew that she was totally in love with this strange, brave, generous man. She was honest enough with herself to admit that a portion of her attraction did come from the fact that he was so well regarded by the community. A leader, a legend, and a close personal friend of The Forever Man, king of the human Free State. After all, power was a great aphrodisiac.

But it was more than that. She saw a side of him that many others did not. Shyness that he hid behind a wall of sarcasm and acerbic wit, his generosity of spirit and his unthinking bravery.

And most of all, his unconscious kindness towards both her and her girls.

He took her hand and raised it to his lips, kissing it lightly. ‘My princess,’ he said.

‘Stop it,’ she laughed. ‘I ain’t no princess.’

‘You are to me,’ replied Tad.

She laughed again and then, looking over Tad’s shoulder, she pulled away and sank into a low curtsey.

‘Your majesty.’

Tad turned around to see Nathaniel approaching.

‘Hey, king,’ he greeted his friend.

‘Yo, Tad,’ answered Nathaniel. ‘Maryanne,’ he continued. ‘I hope that I find you well. All settled in now?’

Maryanne nodded. ‘We are staying at Tad’s house,’ she said. ‘He has made us most welcome.’

‘Good. Maryanne, I need to speak to Tad alone.’

‘Of course, majesty. I’ll take the girls home. It’s time for lunch at any rate.’ She curtsied again and went on her way.

‘What’s up, Nate?’ asked Tad.

‘We’ve had bad news,’ answered the Marine. ‘Our long-range scouts have just come in from the south.’ Nathaniel took a deep breath. ‘The abbey has been destroyed. Axel is dead. They’re all dead.’

Tad went pale. ‘All? Janice, Father O’Hara?’

‘Every single soul. To the last one. Apparently, they took out over five thousand Roaches.’

‘What about the Fair-Folk garrison at Hope Valley?’ asked Tad. ‘There are over twenty thousand Orcs and goblins stationed there. Where were they?’

Nathaniel shook his head. ‘I have sent a message to Commander Ammon of the Fair-Folk to enquire as to what happened. All that we can do is wait for a reply.’

Tad’s face was pinched with anger. ‘That’s not good enough,’ he said. ‘Over three thousand humans died. There is no excuse for that. We must make them pay.’

‘I agree,’ said Nathaniel. ‘But there is nothing that we can do. We’re stretched paper-thin as it is. To declare war against the Fair-Folk, our supposed allies, would be worse than insanity. It would be suicide. For the whole of humanity. We can barely maintain a war on one front, to fight on two would spell the end.’

‘I know,’ said Tad. ‘I’m sorry. It’s just that I feel so damned helpless.’

‘We can only do what we can do,’ said Nathaniel. ‘In the meantime, we must take whatever happiness is offered.’

Tad nodded at the advice and set off home, to Maryanne and the girls.

Gramma Higgins had lived on The Farm, or Harry's Farm as it was known by the humans, for over twenty years now. She had outlived her nieces Janeka and Adalyn, both taken by the cancer. She missed them every day.

Her life on The Farm had been acceptable, she was respected, not asked to do any work, and generally did what she wanted. The only down side is that the humans were totally controlled by the Fair-Folk and their minions. What they did, how and where they lived, their food rations, and their remuneration.

In return, however, they got protection from roving bands of bandits and sundry vagabonds. She had, once or twice, contemplated leaving and escaping to the Free State but after thinking about it she could find no real reason to take the risk.

This morning she had, once again, woken before sunrise as was her habit. She had made herself a cup of bitter acorn coffee, sweetened with honey and then walked out onto her front porch to watch the sun rise.

The first things that she noticed were the Orcs and goblins. They were moving quietly and efficiently, packing handcarts, and loading goods onto each others' backs. She put her mug down and approached the nearest Orc sergeant.

'Sergeant,' she said. 'What de hell be happening?'

The Orc ignored her totally.

Gramma kicked him in the shin. 'Hey, answer me,' she said. 'What going on?'

The Orc, knowing that Gramma would keep kicking him until he answered, decided to capitulate.

'We have been ordered back to London.'

'Who has?'

The Orc swept his hand around. ‘Everyone.’

‘Humans as well?’

He shook his head. ‘No. Only denizens of the Fair-Folk.’

‘Well, what about us?’ asked Gramma. ‘Who will protect us from the Roaches?’

The Orc carried on packing his hand cart. Gramma waited for a while, but it was obvious that the conversation was over.

By now, the sun had risen, and more humans were coming out of their dwellings, children wide-eyed in wonder and adults small-faced with concern.

Murmurs of concern started to ripple through the community as the ranks of Orcs and goblins started to march out of the central farm enclosure. There was no sign of the Fair-Folk farm commander and it soon became obvious that he had already left.

As the warriors left, the humans started to slowly gravitate towards

Gramma, sensing her as their natural leader now that the Fair-Folk were gone.

Eventually, there was a large crowd in front of Gramma's house, standing and staring. Waiting.

'What all you fools doing staring at an old lady,' snapped Gramma.

'What should we do?' asked someone in the crowd.

'What, you people been sheep for so long dat you forgot how to be wolves?' she asked. 'You all forgot how to make a decision yourself, like little chilluns?' She continued, hoping to shame them into some sort of action.

There was a pause and then someone else spoke up. 'Tell us what to do.'

'Yes,' called out others. 'Tell us.'

Gramma shook her head in disgust. 'Truly, you peoples are worse dan slaves. How should I know what to do? I's an ole lady who ain't done naught for over twenty years now.'

'Should we pack up and make for the

Free State?' asked a tall man.

'Or should we stay here and defend the walls?' asked another.

'We should send an emissary to the Annihilators. Sue for peace. We're just farmers. They'll see that and leave us alone.'

'They'll kill us,' yelled a woman.

'Shut it!' shouted Gramma. 'All youse just be quiet.' She cast her angry eye over the crowd. 'You wants to know what to do?' she asked. 'Well den, Gramma will tell you. We's got no chance of making it through a hundred miles of Roach territory to the Free State. Dose insects will catch us and kill us for shore. And you, you fool,' she pointed at the man who had suggested suing for peace. 'You go speak to dose Roaches and ask dem for peace, dey will kill you sooner dan look at you.'

'So, what do we do?' asked the man again.

'We batten down de hatches,' said Gramma. 'We put our people on de wall and we prepare to defend dis place with our lives. Because when dose Roaches come for us dey are not going to stop. Dey will be coming to destroy us.'

The crowd stared at Gramma for a few seconds and then immediately started arguing amongst themselves. Some were for going, some staying and defending the farm, others wanted to follow the Orcs, and still others wanted to do nothing and simply carry on as normal.

'Fools,' said Gramma to herself as she picked up her mug, took a sip and grimaced with distaste. The brew was cold. She went back inside to make a new one.

The crowd didn't notice that she had gone.

She boiled the water and threw the roasted acorn powder into the pot, boiling it vigorously for a few minutes. Then she poured the brew into her mug and spooned in a large quantity of honey. There wasn't much left but there was no reason to conserve it.

She reckoned that the Roaches would be there soon and, when they did—well, she would have no need for honey anymore.

Walking slowly so as not to spill the hot liquid, she went and sat in her favourite chair, leant back to get comfortable.

And waited for the end.

The snow swirled in the air reducing visibility to less than twenty yards.

Tad pulled his cloak tightly around him and squinted as he tried to pierce the veil of churning white flakes.

'There's no one out there,' said Nathaniel with a chuckle in his voice. 'Well, not for a couple of miles at least. I would know.'

'They'll come,' said Tad. 'With the weather like this we lose our air superiority advantage, so they'll come. I guarantee it.'

'I'm sure that they will,' agreed the Marine. 'And when they do, we'll be ready for them. So,' he continued.' How is married life treating you?'

Tad raised an eyebrow. 'I'm not married.'

‘As good as,’ quipped the Marine. ‘As good as.’

‘True,’ admitted The Little Big Man. ‘It’s good. I’m happy. For the first time ever, I am truly happy. I have a family. I feel complete.’

‘And you, Kob, my friend,’ asked Nathaniel of the large Orc standing next to him.

‘I am alive,’ answered the Orc.

‘Yes, that is true,’ confirmed Nathaniel. ‘But, are you happy?’

‘I continue to exist,’ said Kob. ‘I have food enough and water enough, and a place to shelter from the weather when I need it.’

‘So, would you say that you are content?’

‘Every morning I wake to greet a new day, so, yes, I am content.’

‘Well whoop-de-doo,’ said Tad. ‘What verve for life, I almost can’t stand the enthusiasm. Come on, Kob,’ continued The Little Big Man. ‘Crack a smile.’

The Orc stared at Tad for a full

second before he spoke, his face a blank mask.

'I am smiling,' he said, and then turned to carry on staring into the snowstorm.

Suddenly Nathaniel tensed. 'They're coming,' he said. Two miles out or so. Moving fast. Coming straight for us. Lots of them. Maybe more than ten thousand. Heading for the gate.' Then The Forever Man pulled in some of the pulse power around him and used it to enhance his voice so that it boomed out across the wall for all to hear.

'Ready yourselves,' he shouted. 'Annihilators incoming. ETA six minutes. They're coming in fast so brace hard, my bet is that they are not going to do their usual forming up thing and are simply going to hit us at speed.'

The humans waited, and the time ticked by. Minute sized paving stones of pure tension leading to a world of hurt.

The Roaches appeared out of the whiteout, becoming visible as they were almost already at the wall. There was no volley of spears, no sound of war cries. Nothing to give warning. If it had not been for The Forever Man's ability to sense them coming, they would have been over the wall before any human could react.

The archers managed to get off one volley before the ladders were thrown against the wall and the Roaches swarmed up.

It was the most desperate battle that the Free State had ever faced. As fast as they threw the invaders back, pushing the ladders from the wall, the faster they were replaced. It was obvious that this was an all-out push by the Annihilators to coincide with the weather and the lack of air support available to the humans.

Eventually, through sheer force of numbers, a substantial number of Roach warriors made the top of the wall and formed a fighting wedge, driving the human defenders before them as they pushed forward.

Nathaniel pointed at the Roach wedge

with his axe and strode forward, Tad on his right and Kob on his left. The human warriors stood back allowing their king to pass and then falling in behind him as he did so.

Nathaniel and his two friends hit the Roach fighting wedge like a wrecking ball. Within minutes, they had cleared the walls and Nathaniel commanded the other defenders to redouble their efforts to push the ladders away.

Unlike the usual Roach way of attacking, they did not withdraw to regroup after the initial wave had been defeated, they simply kept pushing.

Wave after wave threw themselves at the wall. Hundreds of ladders at a time. Thousands of warriors.

After a couple of hours, the battlements were awash with blood, slippery and treacherous underfoot. Both men and aliens hacked and cut at each other in a frenzy of violence.

Nathaniel conjured up the odd fireball to help clear the walls, striking down

Roaches with burning balls of plasma. But he had to be careful. Such conjuring used up an absurd amount of energy, and if he overused the magiks, he ran the risk of draining himself and succumbing to exhaustion.

'Problem,' shouted Tad and he pointed.

Nathaniel glanced in the direction that The Little Big Man was indicating and saw a Roach warrior that had made the top of the wall. He was different to the other Roaches around him. His armored carapace was predominantly red, and he stood at least a foot taller. His bladed appendages were longer than the usual Roach and he appeared to be heavier built.

Two human defenders ran at the new Roach, swinging their broadswords as they did. The alien warrior dispatched them both with a casual backhand of his bladed appendages. Then he scanned the walls, his head swiveling slowly from left to right. He stopped when his eyes landed on Nathaniel.

'Forever Man,' he bellowed. 'I am Ikara, Busho High Warrior, second only to Supreme Warrior Akimiri Hijiti, and I have come for you.'

Nathaniel smiled but his green eyes glittered with hate. 'And you have found me, High Warrior,' he answered as he strode forward, his double-bladed axe held at the ready.

Humans and Roaches alike scattered out of the path of the two Alpha beings as they approached each other, bent on battle.

The Roach moved first, his blades swinging so fast as to defy human perception. But not superhuman perception.

Nathaniel watched the blades coming and leant back, allowing them to streak past his face. Then he ducked underneath and swung his axe at the Roach's legs. The Busho jumped backwards and struck again.

Nathaniel was impressed. The alien was moving fast. Faster than anyone or anything that The Forever Man had ever come across before. He blocked the cut with his axe blade and kicked out, hitting the Busho on his knee. The Roach staggered back but recovered quickly and slashed out again, nicking Nathaniel on the neck.

The Marine took a step back and regarded the Roach with newfound respect as he felt the hot, sticky redness flow down his neck into his armor. Again, and again, the two warriors attacked each other, and after six or seven clashes it started to become obvious that the Annihilator Busho was hopelessly outclassed.

When Nathaniel pulled back from one clash he glanced quickly around him to see that the battle had stopped. The Annihilators stood still, their bladed appendages by their sides as they watched one of their Supreme Warriors take on the human king. The humans likewise simply stood and watched their leader as he battled the Busho, engrossed by the savage intensity.

Nathaniel waited for the Busho to attack again and then he stepped to one side and launched a lightning series of blows with his axe, striking alternately low and high, over and over again, raining them down at a rate of over four a second.

The Busho went down under the welter of strikes. Blood sprayed high as parts of his carapace shattered under the impact of the winged steel blades.

Finally, Nathaniel kicked the Busho in the chest and knocked him to the floor. Then he stepped over him, raised his axe and severed his head from his body.

A collective groan erupted from the Annihilators and many of them fell to their knees.

One approached Nathaniel, his head down and his demeanor one of respect.

'Great warrior,' he greeted The Forever Man. 'You have defeated one of the paramount warriors of our kind. As befits the occasion we ask that the battle be forestalled for a short moment whilst we remove his body from the field and perform the appropriate funeral rites.'

Nathaniel agreed straight away, happy with the opportunity to consolidate his troops. Augmenting his voice once again he instructed all humans to stand down and let the Annihilators remove their fallen Busho.

Six of the Roaches lifted Ikara onto their shoulders and carried him back, lowering the body down the ladder first. The solemnity of the occasion marred somewhat by the fact that one of the Roaches had to carry the Busho's severed head in a bag. As they walked through the massed ranks of Annihilators the warriors dropped to one knee and saluted, one appendage against their chest.

Then they all formed up and withdrew, fading into the snow storm.

'Quickly,' said Nathaniel to Tad. 'See to the men. Get someone to wash the blood from the walkways, feed and water everyone. Ready the archers.'

Tad grabbed the Marine by the arm. 'Nathaniel,' he said. 'We should attack now. While they're doing whatever the hell it is that they're doing. We could take them by surprise.'

Nathaniel shook his head. ‘No.’

‘Why?’ insisted Tad.

‘Why?’ asked the Marine. ‘Because that’s not what we do. We said that we would stand down while they bury their Busho dude and that is what we will do.’

Tad looked angry. ‘It’s not a time to stand on honor,’ he insisted. ‘We have the human race to think about. Screw honor.’

Nathaniel grinned and then laughed, catching Tad by surprise.

‘What?’ enquired The Little Big Man. ‘Why you smiling like a Cheshire cat and what’s so funny?’

Nathaniel pointed at the sky.

Tad looked up and shrugged. ‘What? There’s nothing up there. Snow, clouds, the sun.’

Nathaniel grinned again, and Tad started to chuckle. ‘The snow is clearing,’ said The Little Big Man.

The Marine nodded. ‘And I have already pulsed our contact in the Vandal camp. I’ve scrambled all of them and told them to pack heavy bombs only. I'm gambling that the Roaches won't get any Yari in the air in time so we won't need fighter protection.'

Tad punched the air. 'Yes. Will they get here in time?'

'They had better,' said Nathaniel. 'Because we're in big trouble if they don't.'

The defenders waited on the wall, nerves strung tight as garroting wire. And above them, over the next three hours, the sky started to clear. Some men simply stood alone, some chatted in groups, others played cards. But they all kept glancing outwards, scanning for the next attack.

Then, as patches of blue became visible and no more snow fell, there was a shout from the watchmen on the wall.

The Annihilators were coming.

The ground trembled in time with the running footsteps of almost fifteen thousand alien feet as they charged towards the wall, hundreds of scaling ladders at the ready.

And then the light faded as if a massive cloud had passed before the sun.

Tad looked up, thinking that the sky was clouding over again. Instead he saw, in V-shaped flights of one hundred, a massed formation of over five thousand Vandals. Every able-bodied flyer had taken to the air.

The humans cheered as the first wave of five hundred ground support Vandals dove towards the Roaches, pulling up some fifty feet above their heads and releasing their naphtha bombs. Each dropping, one, two, three, four. A carpet of fire leapt up amongst the charging Annihilators forcing them to stagger to a halt.

And then the next wave of Vandals struck, and the next, and the next. By the time that the first three thousand Vandals had delivered their payloads the rest were forced to drop their loads from much higher up, such was the fierceness of the conflagration.

The humans merely stood and watched the firestorm. There was nothing else that they could do. Eventually they had to either duck behind the battlements or raise their shields up to protect themselves from the intense waves of heat emanating from the battlefield.

The massive field of fire grew so hot that it started to suck in air from the surrounding atmosphere, creating its own mini-weather system. Small flaming tornados started up, twirling away from the field, and igniting the surrounding trees. Flames shot hundreds of feet into the air, eventually stopping in a huge mushroom-shaped cloud that was torn apart by the stratospheric jet winds.

The armada of Vandals regrouped and flew back to base, heading north.

Behind them, not one Annihilator was left alive.

On the wall, no one spoke for a while. The level of destruction was simply too much to take in straight away.

Eventually Tad spoke. ‘God,’ he said in a shaky voice. ‘That was truly terrible.’

‘It had to be done,’ said Nathaniel.

‘I know,’ admitted Tad. ‘But still. My God.’

‘War is cruelty,’ said The Forever Man. ‘And there is no use trying to change that. The crueler it is, the sooner it will be over.’

‘That is true,’ affirmed Kob. ‘Not only that, we must accept that this time we were lucky. If the weather had not broken I doubt that we would have been able to hold them back. There are simply too many of them. Even this,’ he gestured with his arm. ‘Even this is not such a huge loss to them. I would guess that they still have over fifty thousand warriors left. Maybe even more. To be honest, I do not see how we can keep winning.’

The Forever Man patted the Orc on the shoulder and smiled. ‘Have faith, my friend,’ he said. ‘It’s not over until the fat lady sings.’

The three of them stood in silence for a few minutes as they watched the flames slowly die down.

Finally, Kob spoke again. ‘I do not

know this fat lady,' he said as he turned to leave the wall. 'But I will try to have faith.'

Milly picked another peeled grape from the bowl and looked out over the frozen river. A fire blazed in the hearth, yet she still wore her mink stole. She simply loved the softness of the fur.

A young girl was on her hands and knees scrubbing the stone floor and another stood at the door, simply waiting for instructions.

The table in the center was laid with a selection of candied fruits, peeled grapes, and fruit sherbets. These were Commander Ammon's favorite foods and she had ensured that there were sufficient quantities available, even though it was getting harder and harder to obtain such delicacies in a land that was almost constantly shrouded in snow.

But, as the paramount human in the land of the Fair-Folk, doors were opened to her that would not be opened even to some of the actual Fair-Folk.

She thought about Nathaniel. How he could have had all of this. She had offered it to him on a plate, but he had refused her. And moreover, he had utterly rejected her, casting aspersions on her ambitions and then leaving her again. But the worst thing had been the look of disappointment and pity on his face when he had left. She would far have preferred hatred.

Because, God how she hated him. He was responsible for all of the wrongs that were facing both humanity and the Fair-Folk. His massive arrogance prevented him from bowing down before the Fair-Folk. A race who only wanted to do their best for the humans. A race that ruled with a hand that was strict but fair.

And if Nathaniel had not made such enemies of them, then the whole of humanity and the Fair-Folk would be properly arrayed against the Annihilator invaders. Instead their forces were split.

This resulted in a division of power and an inability to strike a powerful blow.

Nathaniel talked about freedom. Humanity had to be free. But she had experienced freedom before and she knew exactly what it brought. Freedom to rape. Freedom to kill the innocent. Freedom to pillage and destroy. None of that happened under the Fair-Folk. And Nathaniel was too steeped in the ways of war to ever bend a leg to those who should be his true masters and the rulers of the human lands.

The door opened, and the commander walked in. He was still presenting himself to Milly as a six-foot, blond, blue eyed male of indeterminate pre-middle age. As opposed to allowing her to see his four-foot, grey-skinned, domed-head appearance. The attractive appearance helped the Fair-Folk to control the humans, although of late, Ammon was coming to the conclusion that it was no longer really needed. Those who knew the true appearance of the Fair-Folk all currently lived in the Free State, and those who didn't know were either totally subjugated by the Fair-Folk, or so indebted to them as it would make no difference how they looked.

Milly curtsied deeply, and he bowed in return. 'My lady,' he greeted her. 'I have come for some input regarding a plan that Seth and I have formulated.'

'I am honored, Commander,' replied Milly as she showed him to a seat at the table of treats and sweetmeats.

Ammon sat down and helped himself to a piece of honeyed apricot.

At first, he had started coming to visit Milly to ask her input merely because he felt it prudent to allow her the feeling that she was involved in some decisions, bearing in mind that she was the preeminent human in the Fair-Folk realm. But, as time went on, he soon discovered that the human female was a canny thinker and at least as ruthless as he was. She would always manage to parcel her decisions up in a wrapping of concern; a veneer of care for her people, but when push came to shove, it was obvious that

Milly put Milly first and foremost.

The commander accepted a cup of fruit sherbet, sipped, and then spoke.

'Seth and I are thinking about sending an emissary to the Annihilators to sue for peace. What do you think?'

Milly thought for a short while before she spoke. 'What incentive have they got? I mean, on the surface I think that it's a good idea but why would they do it? From what I hear they aren't exactly doing that badly as far as the war goes. What do we have to offer them, they seem to live only for war and conquest?'

Ammon nodded. 'True, although they have just taken a serious beating at the wall. The human king created a firestorm using his Vandals and wiped out over fifteen thousand Annihilators.'

Milly paused as she took the figures in. Fifteen thousand dead. Nathaniel truly was one of the dogs of war. Anyone capable of wreaking such destruction must surely be rooted in evil. 'How many does that leave?' she asked.

'Our scouts reckon that there are still anything from another fifty to a hundred thousand of them. We aren't sure. But, if I am being honest, their warriors are far superior to ours. Our Orcs have proved to be too slow and stolid to fight successfully against them. To ensure a win we would need to outnumber them at least ten to one. I am not being defeatist, merely candid regarding our chances.'

'The humans seem to be faring quite well against them,' commented Milly.

Ammon nodded. 'They haven't done badly, but they have been lucky. I don't think that the full might of the Annihilators has been thrown against them. You see, they still have to leave a substantial number of troops facing our lines in case we attack in strength.'

Milly smiled. She could see where the discussion was heading. 'So,' she said. 'You *do* have something to offer them. You can offer them the Free State.'

Ammon was impressed, as usual, at the human girl's sharp mind. 'Yes,' he affirmed. 'If we guaranteed peace, then the Annihilators could concentrate their forces entirely on the humans and would, no doubt, destroy them completely. We would offer them the country from London north and we would control the rest. It is more than sufficient for our needs.'

'No more war,' added Milly. 'We could run the land without interference from Nathaniel and his armies. Humanity would finally be at peace.'

'A true and everlasting peace,' agreed Ammon.

'I think that you should do it,' urged Milly. 'Moreover, I think that you should send a human emissary. That would show the Annihilators that we truly are a multicultural society, Fair-Folk and humans living together. Benevolent overlords ensuring that the humans live in harmony.'

'I agree,' affirmed commander Ammon and he toasted Milly with his cup.

Then he stood up. 'Milly,' he said. 'There is something else that I have to tell you. Well, perhaps, show you, is more appropriate. You know that we do not allow any mirrors in the Tower of London?'

'Yes,' answered Milly. 'When I last asked you for one you said that I had no need to see my beauty reflected. That was very gallant of you.'

'Yes,' agreed Ammon. 'And that was true. However, it is not the real reason for the no mirror rule. I would like you to take a look at this.'

From his robe Ammon drew a small round mirror. Like a lady's compact mirror. He gave it to Milly who held it up and looked into it.

'It's me,' she said in a puzzled voice. 'It's just a mirror. I don't understand.'

Ammon walked over and stood next to her. 'Tilt the mirror slightly.'

Milly did so, and to her credit, she did not drop it. But she did draw in a sharp intake of breath as she saw what was reflected in the mirror. Gray rubbery skin. A large dome-shaped head. Huge black eyes, no ears or nose, and a spindly, long-armed body.

She whipped her head around to face Ammon and did a double take as she was faced with a tall blond human male.

And then, like the whole world was coming into focus, his body dissolved and reformed as the creature that she had seen in the mirror.

'Oh my God,' she whispered. 'You're an alien.'

Ammon said nothing for a while, allowing Milly time for adjustment. 'Yes,' he affirmed. 'In a manner of speaking. Does that matter?'

'Why the façade?' asked Milly.

'We did it to help us assimilate. We thought that it would be easier to become part of our new world if we blended in. But I ask again—does it matter?'

Milly shook her head. 'No. It truly doesn't matter. It does however prove something to me.'

'What?' asked Ammon.

‘It proves that Nathaniel, as well as being a warmonger is also a racist.’

Tad sat back in his chair and relaxed. There had been a lull in Annihilator activity and Nathaniel had firmly told The Little Big Man to take a few days off. In the past Tad would have argued, maintaining that he was needed on the wall. Insisting that a leader should always be present. But now he jumped at the chance to spend time with Maryanne and the girls. Cocooning himself in their love and affection.

The smell of the large breakfast that Maryanne had cooked that morning still lingered in the air. Ham, eggs, and fresh baked bread. The two girls were at the far end of the room, sitting at the dining table, heads bent over their slates as they practiced their letters.

Outside, he could hear the murmur of

conversation and the odd tinkle of female laughter.

Maryanne was in the herb garden picking rosemary for the roast dinner she was going to cook that night and had obviously struck up a conversation with Tammy, the next-door neighbor and wife of Colonel Parker.

Women thrive on gossip, thought Tad, smiling as he wondered whether he should draw himself a beer. It was still early morning, but he felt that he was entitled to push the boat out a little, after all, it was the first full day off the wall for over three weeks.

He decided against it and stood up to get some water instead. Outside he heard someone shout out. An angry explicative. Perhaps someone had slipped and fallen. Or hit their thumb with a hammer whilst mending the fence. He ignored it and ran the tap until the water was running cold.

More shouting intruded and then a woman's scream. Long and drawn out. A cry of terror.

Tad's blood ran cold and he reacted instantly, dropping his mug, and running for the door, picking up his axe and sword as he did so.

'Stay inside,' he shouted at the two girls. 'Lock the door behind me. Do it.'

He slammed the door as he ran through.

Annihilators!

One of them attacked Tad, slashing at him as he exited the door. The Little Big Man dropped, rolled, and stabbed upwards, piercing the Roach's groin and dropping him in a welter of blood.

Two more approached and Tad cut through them as he fought with total desperation.

'Maryanne,' he shouted as he searched for her.

He looked up and saw groups of Yari flying overhead. Each group of four carried a wicker basket under them and in each basket were two Annihilator warriors. They had obviously flown high over the wall and managed to drop in undetected.

A quick glance around showed him that there were probably two or three hundred Roaches in the near vicinity and they were wreaking havoc on the surprised humans. Cutting down women and children and unarmed farmers.

Tad hacked his way through another attacker and ran to the herb garden around the side of the house.

Maryanne's body lay on the ground, still and broken. Covered in blood.

Tad ran up and knelt next to her, cradling her head in his hands. As he touched her he knew that she was gone. Her body was limp and lifeless. The injuries massive and horrific.

The small pruning knife in her hand was covered in blood and a few feet away lay a single Roach warrior. She had defended herself with valor.

Tears ran down Tad's face as he gently lay Maryanne's head down.

The Little Big man stood up, gathered

his weapons, and went looking for Roaches to kill.

They lost over six hundred humans that day. The majority of them women and children. In return, two hundred Roach warriors were exterminated. Tad killed seventeen.

As a result of the airborne raid, Nathaniel ordered that the Vandals maintained a constant vigil above the villages behind the wall, further stretching their limited resources, and adding to their exhaustion.

Humanity tottered on the very edge of existence.

Papa Dante managed to smile. 'Good of you to come,' he croaked.

Nathaniel grasped Papa's hand and squeezed gently. 'You look terrible,' he said.

'Good,' replied Papa. 'If I felt this bad and still looked my usual dashing self then people wouldn't feel sorry for me.' He coughed weakly and then grimaced as the small movement wracked his body with pain. 'The wall is almost finished,' he said. 'Roo is still out there, pushing the men to put the finishing touches. I told you that we could do it.'

'I never doubted you, old friend,' said Nathaniel. 'Not for a second. Now rest. No more talking.'

Papa grinned again, although it was

hard to tell if it was humor or a grimace of pain. 'I need to talk,' he said. 'Don't have much time left. Is Sam here?'

A young man stepped forward. He was broad of shoulder, narrow of hip. His eyes were the blue of a stormy ocean, his hair as black as crude oil, his jaw strong and pugnacious. He took Papa's hand.

'I am here, Papa,' he said, his voice gruff with hidden emotion.

'Young Somhairle,' whispered Papa. 'Do you remember when I first found you?'

Sam nodded. 'I was hiding in a hedge and your horse stuck its head in and snorted at me. I thought that it was a monster and I was going to be torn to shreds.'

Papa chuckled. 'Dancer. Her name was Dancer.'

Sam nodded in agreement. 'And then you took me in,' he continued. 'You gave me a family. You gave me a new name.' Finally, a single tear slid down Sam's face, belying his stoical expression.

Papa struggled to sit up, grunting in agony as he did so.

Sam tried to push him back down. ‘No, Papa,’ he said. ‘Rest.’

‘No, Somhairle,’ he argued. ‘I need to be sitting up for this. Now listen. All of you,’ the dying man gestured for all to come closer.

Mama, Nathaniel, Gogo, and Sam all drew in around the bed.

‘Sam,’ he said. ‘Do you know my name?’

Sam nodded. ‘Papa Dante.’

Papa shook his head. ‘No, that’s just what everybody calls me. My name is Durante Breathnach. My father was Connor Breathnach, he was known as Papa Connor. My grandfather, Gwennin Breathnach, known as Papa Gwennin.’ Papa took a shuddering breath. ‘Now, Sam my boy. I have no heir, so I give you the title. Papa Sam.’

Sam frowned. ‘I’m not sure what that means.’

'It means that you are now the leader of the Walking People,' said Gogo. 'You are our father. Papa Sam.' Gogo bowed. '*Tá muid do sheirbhísigh*,' she said.

Mama stood forward and bowed as well. '*Tá muid do sheirbhísigh*. We are your servants.'

Sam said nothing, he simply sat next to Durante and held his hand, his face an expressionless block of granite disproved by the glitter of emotion that filled his eyes.

After much discussion, the Fair-Folk, in conjunction with human Milly, had decided to send Lord Bartholomew Richards to the Annihilators to act as their emissary.

Bartholomew was a man of advancing middle age. Before the pulse his father was a lord, and on his death, Bartholomew had inherited the title. He insisted on using it on any possible occasion, even though his estate was owned by a member of the Fair-Folk, and Bartholomew lived in a two-roomed house, fit for those with little or no discernable skills in the post-pulse world.

People did still call him Lord and he had convinced himself that the title was used as a sign of respect as opposed to the indication of mockery that it actually was.

It was this very ability to assume his own superiority and preeminence in the face of the obvious that prompted Milly to forward him as a choice. She maintained that he had just enough confidence and self-importance to deliver the Fair-Folks' message with sincerity and aplomb.

But none of that mattered now.

'So,' said Commander Ammon. 'How was it delivered?'

'A Yari dropped it on one of our outlying encampments,' answered the Orc who was standing to attention opposite the commander.

'When?'

'This morning, Commander. Just after first light.'

Ammon sighed. 'Fine. You can go.'

The Orc saluted and turned on his heel.

'Wait,' said Ammon. 'Take it with you. I certainly have no use for it.'

'Of course, Commander,' responded the Orc as he grabbed Lord Bartholomew's severed head and left the room.

Tad let the empty bottle drop from his fingers and fall to the flagstone kitchen floor. It shattered with a sharp pop and the shards littered the floor like frozen tears.

He pulled another bottle towards himself and fumbled drunkenly with the cork for a while. Eventually, he pulled the stopper using his teeth and spat it onto the floor to join the rest of the filth and detritus.

The Little Big Man took a deep pull on the brandy and shuddered, wondering how long it took to literally drink yourself to death. Two days? Three? Four? No, he thought, longer. Must be, because he had been drinking like this for almost a week now, and although he felt like death, he continued to breathe.

After Maryanne's death he hadn't left the kitchen except to relieve himself or to find more alcohol.

Tammy, the next-door neighbor, had taken in Clare and Stephanie. She had brought them across to visit a couple of times, but Tad had refused to open the door, choosing instead to wallow in his own terrible misery.

Tad took another pull on the bottle and then started as the front door slammed open.

Gogo stormed into the room, negotiating her way around the furniture and litter in spite of her lack of sight. She walked straight up to Tad, drew back her hand and slapped his face hard enough to pitch him off his chair and onto the floor.

The Little Big Man simply lay there. Unmoving. He didn't even bother to raise a hand to his face.

'Get up,' yelled the old lady.

Tad rose to his knees and then, wobbling slightly as he did so, to his feet. He stared at Gogo, his face a mask of insane grief.

'What?' he asked in a croaking whisper.

'How dare you?' said Gogo. 'You selfish, stupid man. Maryanne is dead. Dead.'

Tad flinched as she spoke, each word cutting into his soul like a blade.

'The dead have no feelings,' continued Gogo. 'The dead don't wallow in self-pity. The dead cannot take care of anyone. They are dead.' She slapped Tad again and this time he rubbed his cheek.

'Oh good,' said Gogo. 'You felt that one, did you?'

Tad nodded and then sat down on the chair again. As he did so he noticed, for the first time, that Clare and Stephanie were standing behind Gogo.

The old blind lady beckoned to them. 'Step forward, little ones,' she said. 'Come and greet your father.'

Both of the girls came and stood next to Tad, putting their arms around him as they did.

'Gogo says that mommy won't be coming back,' said Stephanie.

Tears ran down Tad's face. 'I'm so sorry, my darlings,' he said.

'Why?' asked Clare.

'I couldn't save her,' sobbed Tad. 'She was my everything, and I couldn't save her.'

'We know,' said Clare. 'But you tried.'

'Yes,' admitted Tad. 'God how I tried.'

The three of them sat together for a while, arms around each other.

Eventually Stephanie spoke. 'You smell,' she said. 'Why don't you go and take a bath, and Clare and I will make something to eat?'

Tad stood up and nodded. 'I think that would be great,' he said. 'Thank you.'

He turned to thank Gogo as well, but she had gone, and the door was closed. It was as if she had never been there.

Papa Dante's body had been washed, shaven, and wrapped in pure white linen before being placed in his casket. The casket was then laid out in the open, surrounded by the vardos, or wagons, of the walking folk.

Torches were lit and placed at his head and feet, and spares were placed ready to light, so that there was always living flame around him during the entire period of the wake.

Over a thousand people had lined up to pay their respects and were wending their way past the coffin, each one kneeling, crossing themselves and mumbling a quick prayer.

On the far side of the circle, the walking people had erected three whole oxen on the spit and they rotated above a long bed of coals. The spits were driven by a group of boys who took turns to grind the handles and slowly rotate the meat.

Next to the roasting oxen were two long tables laden with food and drink. Potatoes, fresh baked bread, vegetables, casks of ale, mead, and flagons of brandy.

On the outside of the circle of Vardos burned a massive bonfire, its flames leaping high into the frigid night sky. Orange and yellow dancers, their arms stretching high above the tree tops. Burning supplicants pleading with the gods, trying to reach the heavens before they died and turned to ash.

The feasting and drinking would continue all night and into the next day as the mourners both paid their respects and celebrated his life and achievements.

As was tradition, many of the men stood around Papa Dante's body smoking their pipes, the fragrant tobacco smoke wreathing the area like early morning mist. It was reputed that the smoke would keep the evil spirits away and allow Papa's soul free access to paradise.

There would be no eulogy, no impassioned speeches, no public outpourings of grief. The wake would be conducted with dignity and reverence, and once the sun had risen the next day, the mourners would accompany the body to its final resting place where it would be buried. A silver cross would be placed in his hands, the casket would be sealed, and he would be laid beneath the sod. A simple stone would mark the grave. His name, date of birth, and of death. Nothing else.

Nathaniel stood alone in the shadows next to one of the Vardos. He thought of Axel and his wife, Janice. The Prof, Father O'Hara. Gramma Higgins, her two nieces, Janeka and Adalyn. Maryanne. There were countless others as well. Men, women, and children. Kings, and peasants, and warriors, Marines, civilians.

Janiver, his queen when he was king of the Picts. Torkill, his druid. Padraig his most trusted friend and Lord of the Lance who had betrayed him with Janiver.

Now Papa Dante. The pain of relationships lost and found. How many more could he bear to lose? How many more people that he loved would he outlive?

A voice spoke to him, speaking to him without words. The voice of the Unicorn. 'You are The Forever Man,' it said.

And he knew the answer. Everyone. He would outlive everyone that he ever loved. He would spend eternity losing all that was dear to him. Over and over, and over again. A thousand lifetimes of bereavement.

He sensed someone next to him and turned to look. It was Gogo. She held out a mug to him and he took it. Brandy. And something else, some sort of herb or spice. He took a sip and the warmth spread through his body, melting the ice that seemed to have encased his heart and stoking the fires of his spirit.

'Thank you, Gogo.'

'Papa Dante is the fourth leader of the walking people that I have buried,' she said.

‘Does it get any easier?’ asked Nathaniel.

‘I wish that it did,’ said Gogo.

The two stood in silence for a while, watching the line of mourners pay their respects.

‘I don’t know if I can handle it,’ said Nathaniel. His voice a quiet whisper.

‘You can,’ said Gogo. ‘Because you have to. You are the lever that tilts the world. Without you there can be no Alpha or Omega. You are The Forever Man.’

And the torches burned, and the smoke wreathed, and Papa Dante’s soul departed.

It was two days after Papa Dante's funeral and Sam simply needed to be alone. The shock of Papa's death, combined with him being made the new leader of the walking people had left him confused, and quite frankly, overwhelmed.

So, he had packed his saddle bags, mounted his horse and rode, heading for the mountain area of Braemar. It had been a long time since he had been on his own. In fact, it had been a while since he had last had any free time whatsoever. And now that he looked back at the past few months it was obvious that Papa Dante had been grooming him for his position of leadership. He had been running twenty-four-seven, doing all of the tasks that Papa Dante usually did, leaving Papa to concentrate on the new wall.

He had given advice on family disputes, given his blessing to marriages, taken charge of the food distribution, assisted Gogo with new born naming ceremonies and generally kept the cogs of the walking people's community spinning without interruption.

He laughed to himself as he realized how smoothly Papa Dante had passed the reins over to him without him even noticing it. So much for being a perceptive leader, he thought to himself.

Sam had no fixed agenda and no place specific to go. He had allowed himself two nights and three days to sort through his feelings and prepare himself for the next chapter of his life.

That night he erected a small bivouac, stretching a length of canvas between two small trees, fashioning three walls out of packed snow and building a fire at the entrance.

Before he crawled in to his blankets for the night he sat outside of his bivouac and simply stared at the stars. Ever since he was a small boy it had been one of his favorite things to do. He would take a blanket out into the back yard, lie on his back, and stare upwards into the perpetuity of space. Countless billions of suns surrounded by trillions of planets. An infinity of possibility.

He had wondered if that was where the Fair-Folk had come from. Or the Vandals, or the Annihilators. But when he had asked Gogo, she had told him that it wasn't that simple. It was obviously true that the aliens had come from different planets, but Gogo maintained that they had also come from different times, and probably, different dimensions.

Sam struggled to get his head around the concept that the invaders may have come from the future or a parallel universe. He found it much easier to simply think of them as alien raiders and leave it at that.

What worried Sam the most was the simple question of, when would it all end? If the pulse light had opened gateways that allowed these otherworldly beings through, would humanity ever be left in peace? If they somehow managed to defeat and exterminate the Fair-Folk and the Annihilators, what would prevent another nation of would-be rulers from appearing and attempting to subjugate humanity?

Sam stood up and went to his bivouac. Time to sleep, he told himself. No more worrying about the maybes and the might-have-beens. Tomorrow he would wake early, spend the day traipsing around the mountains, and then head home and accept his responsibilities as the new leader of the walking people.

The next day, he woke with the sun and ate a basic breakfast of bread and cheese before he mounted up and headed up the trail, heading for the near summits. After an hour of easy riding his mount started to limp, so Sam dismounted and checked the horse's hooves. When he picked up its back right leg the horse kicked out in reaction against the pain and its hoof caught Sam in the stomach. The blow lifted the young man off the ground and sent him flying through the air and down the side of the mountain. He tried to tuck into a ball to protect himself as he rolled but then he struck a rock, and all went black.

By the time that Sam came to, the sun had passed its zenith and was heading towards the horizon, ready to sign off another day. He slowly worked his way through each limb and then felt his ribs, checking for breaks. There didn't seem to be any overt fractures, merely massive bruising and the odd cut and abrasion.

He stood up, took a deep breath, and winced at the pain.

'Oh well,' he said to himself. 'Let's see if we can find that stupid horse.'

The new leader of the walking people, Papa Sam, staggered zombie-like up the side of the mountain, slipping and sliding on the snow and ice, heading for the trail. Half way up he stopped. And stared. Cut into the side of the slope was a great steel door. Ten feet high and six feet wide, a surface patina of red-brown rust. In the center a large keyhole. Above that, two capital letters stamped into the steel. WD.

Sam had no idea what they stood for.

He kicked on the door a couple of times, but it didn't budge. Next, he took out his dagger and tried to slide it in between the door jamb and the lock, but the fit was too tight. Intrigued but defeated, he decided to get home and tell Roo about the door.

He wasn't sure why, but it just seemed as though it may contain something that might be of interest. After all, one didn't build a massive steel door in the side of a mountain merely to conceal someone's holiday home in the hills.

He clambered up the rest of the slope, and to his amazement, his horse was still there.

He stared at it for a while. 'Asshole,' he said.

The horse whinnied and then looked away sheepishly.

Sam went over and raised its back leg again, making sure that he kept a tight hold on it. There was a small pebble trapped in the horse's frog and he flicked it out using the point of his dagger.

'There,' he said to the animal. 'No need to go around kicking me. You're all better now.' He swung up into the saddle. 'Let's go home.'

They trotted off down the trail.

He got back before nightfall and it didn't take long to find Roo and tell him of the door.

Roo scratched his head. A sure sign that he was thinking. 'WD stands for War Department,' he said. 'That would be the Second World War. If my history hasn't completely left me and my memory serves me right, I think that there was a commando training camp in the Braemar Hills during the war. Mountain training to be precise. Could be some sort of storage room. Ammo dump, supplies, that sort of thing. Might just be classified papers. Who knows? Well worth a look,

though. Why don't we get a few lads, some spades and sledgehammers, and you take us back there tomorrow, young Sam. We'll smash our way in and take a look.'

Sam nodded and headed for bed, his battered body crying out for sleep.

He woke the next day as stiff as a corpse in rigor mortis, but Roo was already banging on his door so there was no time for any luxuries like a hot bath and a long breakfast. It was simply a bite to eat, a mug of water, and back in the saddle.

The small column of six men took a few hours to reach the place where Sam had been kicked down the mountain, and they all dismounted and clambered down the steep slope.

Roo took a cursory look at the door. 'No chance of breaking through this,' declared the old Australian. 'It's sealed up tighter than a duck's bum. Better that we dig in to the side of it. It'll be set in concrete but that will be at well over a hundred years old. Concrete deteriorates so we'll have a good chance of smashing through it. That's how we'll get in.'

He instructed the four men that had come with them, and then he and Sam stood back and watched and waited as they stripped off the turf and earth to expose the concrete. Then they set at the barrier with their sledgehammers, striking in rhythm until bits of the old gray material started to crumble and fall off.

Two hours of hard manual labor later, they had opened a hole big enough to squeeze through. Roo collected six torches from the saddle bags, distributed them, lit them, and then led the way into the man-made cave.

The massive door belied the size of the room behind it. It was a standard height room, about ten feet high, and large enough to just fit the three ten seater tables. The tables were covered with dust but had nothing else on them. Ten chairs were placed neatly around each of the tables.

Another room led directly off the first, cutting deeper into the mountain. This room had rows of triple bunk beds bolted to the walls. Enough beds for thirty people. The next room looked like a store room of some sort.

Sam pried open a few boxes with his

dagger. Some of the contents were familiar to him, some not so much. Blankets, uniforms, binoculars, cooking utensils. There were also crates of tins. Sam vaguely remembered tinned food from when he was a small boy. Baked beans in particular. His mother used to make beans on toast for breakfast. Sometimes she would grate food on top of it. But that was then. And, try as he might, he couldn't actually remember what she looked like.

But tinned food had run out many years ago, so he had no recollection of exactly what they looked like. Or tasted like.

Roo picked out a couple of tins and smiled.

'Spam,' he said. 'Steak and kidney, franks and beans.' He laughed. 'Good old war issue food,' he laughed. 'Solid enough to stick to your stomach lining and substantial enough to keep you going all day.'

'Can you still eat that?' asked Sam.

'Yep,' answered Roo. 'Well not ones

like this.' He picked up a tin that had swollen up, the ends as rounded as a baseball. 'That means that it's gone off. But the rest will be fine, not that I'd recommend eating them. I mean, you can live off them, but they taste like crap.'

Sam laughed, and the rest of the men joined in.

Roo held his torch up and looked around the room. 'There,' he pointed at the side of the room. A steel door was set into the wall. A large hasp and staple and padlock secured it shut.

'Jonno,' said the Australian. 'Take a few swings at that padlock with your sledgehammer. Let's see what's inside.'

Jonno hefted his sledgehammer and smashed it into the padlock. But it was a large chunk of steel, so he had to strike it a few more times before it sprung open and fell to the floor.

Sam pulled the door open and Roo stepped inside. He whistled, a long, drawn out exclamation of surprise.

'What is it?' asked Sam.

‘We are going to have to get hold of Nathaniel,’ said Roo. ‘And I mean as quickly as humanly possible. He is definitely going to want to see this.’

Nathaniel stood by the fireplace and stared into the flames. ‘Fire is a truly amazing thing,’ he said. ‘It’s almost like it’s alive. If you’re ever alone and you light a fire, then you have company. It keeps you warm, protects you from wild animals, cooks for you, keeps insects at bay.’

‘Yeah,’ agreed Tad. ‘And if it irritates you, you can pee on it and it goes away.’

The side of Nathaniel’s mouth twitched up in what might have been the beginnings of a smile. ‘Sick, dude.’

‘Sorry,’ apologized Tad. ‘It’s just that you were starting to come over all maudlin. I was just trying to snap you out of it.’

‘Not much chance of that,’ said Nathaniel. ‘Tad,’ he continued. ‘The reason that I have asked you to come here and talk, without any of The Ten or the officers, is that I need to lay things on the line.'

'Go ahead.'

'Look, I'm not going to pull any punches. The Vandals are out on their feet. Or wings, I suppose would be more accurate. The thing is, with the constant air patrols they aren't getting time to rotate out and get rest. Chief Cha-rek has told me that they simply can't keep it up. Some of them are literally collapsing from exhaustion. I don't think that we have fully appreciated the strain that they are under. Mental as well as physical.'

The Marine took a swig from the mug in his hand. It was brandy, rough and strong, and he had to swallow hard to stop himself coughing.

'The same can be said of our troops,' he continued. 'Constant vigilance on the wall is taking its toll. The waiting eats away at their determination, and the constant attacks eat away at their numbers. We simply can't keep taking the sort of casualties that we are. It is unsustainable.'

'So, what do you recommend that we do?' asked Tad, confident that his king would have formulated a plan of some sort.

Nathaniel didn't answer, and when Tad looked at him he noticed the dark rings under his friend's eyes. The hollowness of his cheeks. The general raggedness of his appearance. He was a man wracked by exhaustion. A man who had pushed himself to his physical limits and beyond.

And the Little Big Man cursed himself for being so selfish. For wallowing so deeply in his own self-pity that he had not even noticed that his best friend, and the leader of his people, was literally working himself to death.

'I don't know,' whispered Nathaniel. 'If the Fair-Folk had kept their side of the bargain and had entered the fray with at least some vigor, then we might have been in a better position. As it is, they do the bare minimum to ensure their own survival and we take the brunt of the Annihilator's attacks. We are running low on weapons and food. Even stone to repair the wall.'

The Marine sat down, and his head sank to his chest. 'I do not know what to do,' he said. His voice raw with emotion. 'I have failed.'

There was a frantic banging on the front door.

'Tell them to go away,' said Nathaniel.

Tad walked over to the front door and opened it. Roo barreled into the room, his face wreathed in smiles, his demeanor that of a child before Christmas.

'Look, Roo,' said Tad. 'It's not the best time. I think that you should come back later.'

The Australian shook his head. 'No way, my little mukka. Now is the time and here is the place. This is important, and the king man is going to be chuffed to bits, I promise.'

'It's okay,' said Nathaniel. 'Let him in, it looks like there's no way that he's going to take no for an answer anyway.'

‘Too darn right, king,’ said Roo.

‘So, what is it?’ asked Nathaniel.

Roo shook his head. ‘Can’t tell you,’ he said, the same pleased expression plastered all over his face. ‘You gotta see it yourself. Trust me, this is good news.’

Nathaniel, who had known the Australian for many years now, knew that he was as stubborn as a pile of rocks and if this was the way that he wanted to play things, then this was the way that it would go. He could outright command him using his rank, but even that would probably take almost as long and end up being endlessly more unpleasant. Instead he simply grabbed his axe and his cloak and followed him outside.

His horse was already saddled and was being held by Sam, the new leader of the walking people. A group of fully armed warriors were arrayed behind Sam. The king’s escort.

‘If we ride at a fast trot and keep going into the night we can get there by midday tomorrow,’ said Roo. ‘I have already organized supplies. I have told General Parkinson and he will ensure that the wall is covered. Tad can take over all tactical necessities while you are gone, sire,' finished the Australian as he actually allowed a little respect to color his delivery.

'Lead on, Roo,' commanded the Marine. 'Let's get this party started. Tad, I'll see you in a few days. Try to keep us all alive while I'm gone.'

Tad threw a loose salute and gave a sardonic grin. 'I'll do my best, king,' he said. 'Don't you worry about me. I'll just wait here, not knowing what the hell is going on. Not curious at all, that's me.'

Nathaniel, Roo, and Sam mounted, and the small column trotted off in the direction of the Braemar Hills.

As Roo had suggested, they moved at a fast trot, riding into the night, fortunate for the half-moon that provided just enough light it reflected off the snow.

They grabbed a few hours' sleep, wrapped in their furs next to a small camp fire, and rose the next day to cheese and bread and water, climbing into their saddles as soon as they had eaten.

Nathaniel knew better than to ask Roo where, or even why, they were going. The Australian's sense of theater would keep him mute, and as well as that, Nathaniel knew that it would frustrate Roo even more if he didn't ask, and instead assumed a bored and uninterested demeanor.

'So,' said Roo. 'I suppose that you're wondering where we're going?'

Nathaniel shrugged as if it were the last thing that he was wondering.

'Can't tell you,' said Roo. 'But it'll be worth the wait.'

'Whatever,' mumbled Nathaniel as he pretended to be thinking of something else.

'It's a huge surprise,' continued Roo. 'Come on, why don't you try and guess?'

'Maybe later,' answered Nathaniel, as he tried to hide his grin.

'No,' said Roo. 'We'll be there later. Guess now. You'll never get it. Never

ever.'

'Alright,' sighed the Marine. 'You've discovered a Push-me-pull-you.'

'What?'

'A Push-me-pull-you.'

'What the hell is that?' asked Roo irritably.

'It's a mythical animal with a head on both side of its body,' answered Nathaniel. 'So, when it needs to go anywhere, the one head has to agree with the other whether it should push or pull. If they can't agree, then it can't go anywhere. Push-me-pull-you.'

Roo thought for a while and then he shook his head. 'No. Not possible.'

'Why?' asked Nathaniel.

'If it had a head on each side of its body then how would it take a crap? Not possible.'

For the first time in a while Nathaniel laughed out loud.

'So,' continued Roo. 'Guess again.'

Nathaniel shook his head. 'I'll wait, Roo.'

They continued trotting towards their destination, everyone silent except for Roo who mumbled under his breath about spoilsports and kings and killjoys.

Nathaniel grinned to himself. Roo had the mind of a genius wrapped inside the social graces of a ten-year-old.

And then The Forever Man simply concentrated on riding his horse, allowing himself a few moments of inner peace. A few moments of escape from the grind and stress of leadership.

A few hours later, just before midday, Sam called a halt to the column and dismounted. Everyone followed him as he grabbed a torch from his saddlebag and started to clamber down the mountain.

They got to the door and Sam stood back and ushered Nathaniel in.

Before they had left to fetch the king, Roo and Sam and his men had unpacked a few of the contents from the boxes in the back room and laid them out on the dining tables. Then they had stacked the rest of the cases on the side, against the walls.

Nathaniel stopped dead in his tracks, his mouth hanging open like an industrial fly catcher. Then he strode up to the table and picked one of the items up.

It still smelled of oil and the torchlight reflected off the curved magazine and the length of the blue-black barrel. The Marine racked the receiver back to check. Inside gleamed the gold of a cartridge. It was fully loaded.

It was a Bren light machine gun, circa 1942. A curved magazine carrying twenty rounds of .303 military hardball ammunition.

The Marine looked up at Roo. His astonishment had changed to pure delight.

'There's more,' said Roo as he pulled a sheet of canvas off an item that had been mounted on the floor next to the table.

It was a Vickers heavy machine gun with a two hundred and fifty round canvas belt feed. Also .303 hardball and capable of spitting out five rounds a second and doing so all day without jamming, provided the water-cooled jacket was kept full. In the Second World War two British soldiers with one Vickers had fought off an entire Japanese attack, killing over two hundred men. It was old and the ammunition not as high velocity as more modern weapons had been, but it was still death incarnate.'

Roo handed Nathaniel a hand-written list. 'Here,' he said. 'It's an inventory. And I've checked it all. It all works. Just needs a bit of cleaning and going through the ammo to see if any has had any water ingress and such what.'

The Marine looked at the list.

25 x Thompson machine guns

25 x Colt 45 pistols

5000 x .45 rounds for the Colts and the Thompsons

4 x Vickers machine gun 303 250 round canvas belts

200 belts of 303 (50000 rounds)

6 x Bren light machine guns 303

5000 rounds for the Brens

4 x 3-inch medium mortars

80 x mortar bombs HE

25 x Sten guns 9mm

5000 x rounds 9mm

144 x fragmentation grenades, Mills bombs.

The Marine's brain totaled up the quantities. It was enough ordnance to arm almost one hundred men.

One hundred men armed with modern firepower and sufficient ammunition against bladed weapons and Iron Age missiles.

The Forever Man walked over to Sam and Roo and threw his arms around them. 'Gentlemen,' he said. 'Let's get this stuff back to my place ASAP. We've got some planning to do and some serious butt to kick.'

Roo laughed. 'Told you that you'd be pleased,' he said.

Nathaniel laughed with him. 'And then some, my Australian beauty, and then some.'

The first thing that Nathaniel did when he got home was to send out scouts on horses to canvas all of the villages and hamlets in the Free State. He wanted any male with pre-pulse military experience to report ASAP to headquarters under specific order of the king.

While they were waiting, he and Roo and seven local men who had served in the British pre-pulse army, stripped and tested all of the weapons. They test fired a few rounds from each case and exploded one hand grenade and one mortar round.

Within three days, one hundred and twenty-six men had reported. Their ages varied between forty-seven and eighty-four years of age. Nathaniel personally interviewed everyone and then separated them into groups.

The younger ones that could ride horses he allocated to the Thompson machine guns, the Sten guns and the Colt 45 pistols. They would be the armed cavalry.

The few men that had experience with artillery were assigned to the mortar squad.

Finally, he put the slightly older, more patient men into the machine gun teams. Five to each Vickers, a shooter, feeder, and water jacket filler, and three reloaders to charge the canvas belts with fresh ammunition.

Three to each Bren, one shooter, one to reload and change barrels, and the final to charge the magazines.

The grenades were allocated to the Vandal ground support flyers to augment their fire bombs.

Due to the fact that there was limited ammunition, Nathaniel kept actual firing practice to minimum, concentrating instead on stripping and cleaning the weapons and learning how to clear any jams and avoid overheating. He relied on the fact that all of the men had been trained by the pre-pulse British army, and on the whole, still remembered very well how to fire a weapon, albeit not something hailing from the early 1940s.

After a period of intensive training, the Marine put together a small squad consisting of one Vickers machine gun team, one Bren team, two Thompson soldiers, two Sten gun soldiers, and one mortar team. Fifteen men in all. Excluding him, Tad, and Kob.

To this, he added two hundred cavalry, five hundred foot soldiers, and five hundred Vandals as escorts.

Then he sent the word via a team of fast scout riders, to Commander Ammon of the Fair-Folk, telling him that he was coming to London to discuss the next step in the war against the Annihilators. He would be there, he said, in under a week.

The next morning, they rode out with the rising of the sun. A relatively small column of men. But undeniably the most powerful collection of force that had been seen since the pulse.

They made good time traveling through what was extensively enemy territory. They stuck mainly to the deep forest whenever possible and the vandals walked, only flying every now and then to check out the prevailing landscape to see if any Annihilators were close.

Two days' travel from London they were met by a Fair-Folk detachment. Three thousand Orcs and two thousand goblin archers. The Orc sergeant told Nathaniel that they were there for their protection. Nathaniel said nothing, although it was quite obvious that they were there to ensure that The Forever Man had come in peace and not in sufficient numbers to actually attack.

If the Orcs noticed the odd weapons that some of the humans were carrying they did not mention it. Probably because they had absolutely no idea what they were. For all that they knew they were simply rather complex metal clubs. Also, Orcs have no form of curiosity or imagination, so they just ignored that which they did not comprehend.

By the time they got to the Tower of London where the Fair-Folk commander resided, the column had become a moving fair. A traveling circus. Thousands of humans, mainly children, had joined the march and were skipping and gamboling beside the column. Girls blew kisses at the Free State warriors and cast bold eyes. Older men smoked their pipes and looked on with misty eyes, remembering when all humans were free and wondering how they had ended up as mere vassals of the Fair-Folk.

Rows of substantial tents were set up on the green outside the Tower walls, and Nathaniel and his men were ushered to them.

The Fair-Folk ambassador who had met them explained that the Tower, although large, was not of sufficient size to house Nathaniel and all of his entourage. And as a result, the Fair-Folk had built a tent city outside the walls to house them.

Nathaniel said nothing, and he was

ushered to his specific tent, one much larger than all of the others, so large, in fact, as to be more a canvas house than an actual tent. It was unbelievably sumptuous. The floors were covered in silk carpets, the walls lined in furs, and the furnishings large and comfortable. Coal braziers burned all around the dwelling and the smoke was cleverly funneled out via a series of steel chimneys.

'Wow!' exclaimed Tad. 'These rubber heads know how to live.'

'Yeah,' agreed Nathaniel. 'I am sure that they pulled out all the stops. Showing us how superior they are. Trying to make us feel like the poor relatives. Well it won't work,' he continued. 'It takes more than a few soft furnishings to impress us.'

'Hey,' called Tad, who was standing at a table that was covered in foodstuffs, candies and cakes, and breads and fruits. Roasts and potatoes and steaming piles of vegetables. 'Check it.' He held up a bottle.

Nathaniel walked over. And then stopped. 'Is that sealed?' he asked.

The Little Big Man nodded and handed it over.

Nathaniel slowly unscrewed the top of the bottle. Then he punctured the foil seal and, reverentially, took in a deep breath, savoring the heady, rich smell.

He read the label. 'Barista Style Instant Coffee. Gold Blend.' He laughed out loud. 'Okay,' he admitted. 'Consider me impressed. Let's get some water on the boil and have the first cup of coffee that I have had for over twenty years. Hundreds if you count things in a strictly chronological order.'

Tad found a small iron pot, filled it with water and put it onto one of the braziers. A soon as it came to the boil, Nathaniel piled two heaped spoons of coffee into two pottery mugs and filled them with water.

Then they both sat down and sipped at the dark, bitter beverage, looks of absolute contentment on both of their faces.

Orc Sergeant Kob walked into the tent and looked at the two humans sitting in their chairs and looking as if life couldn't get any better. He sniffed the air, picking up the unfamiliar scent of coffee. Then he stared at their mugs, seeing the dark brown liquid.

'Oh,' he said. 'Is that chocolate?'

'No,' answered Nathaniel. 'It's coffee.'

'What's it made of?' enquired Kob.

The Marine shrugged. 'Some sort of bean.'

'Like chocolate,' said the Orc.

'I suppose so,' admitted Nathaniel.

'Smells awful,' said Kob. 'Commander Ammon is outside. He asks your permission to enter so that you can talk.'

'Send him in,' said Tad.

The commander walked in with another member of the Fair-Folk close behind him.

'Humans,' he greeted. 'This is Seth Hil-Nu, senior mage and my closest advisor.'

Nathaniel stood and introduced himself. 'Marine Master Sergeant Nathaniel Hogan. This is Tad, my right-hand man.'

The Fair-Folk had not bothered to attempt to glamour Nathaniel or Tad as they were well aware that The Forever Man was unaffected by their magiks.

'I notice, your highness,' said Ammon. 'That you introduce yourself as a lowly sergeant when you are a king and a leader of a people. Why is that so?'

'First and always a Marine,' answered Nathaniel. 'God before Corps, Corps before king. I've paraphrased but I'm sure that you get the picture.'

'I am not sure that I understand. But, be that as it may, we have much to discuss. I am sorry to push so hard, I realize that there are the traditional niceties to observe, but perhaps we can do things in reverse and get down to brass tacks first.'

Nathaniel shook his head. 'No.'

Both Ammon and Seth stared at The Forever Man. It was difficult to gauge expression on the alien faces, but their surprise was such that it was visibly reflected on their faces.

'I'm sorry,' ventured Commander Ammon.

'Commander,' said Nathaniel. 'Any plans that you have, anything that you want to say will be proven meaningless until you have seen a few things that I need to show you. Trust me; I am sure that you want to get right into your reasons as to why you cannot fully support any overt action against the Annihilators, how you need to protect your borders and so on and whatever. But after you have seen my display all will change. So, I say to you—No. We shall put off all talks until tomorrow.'

There was a long silence as Ammon and Seth stared at Nathaniel and struggled to adjust their thinking.

Finally, Ammon asked. 'What display?'

‘Well now,’ said Tad. ‘We need to ask a favor of you, Mister Commander dude.’

Ammon gestured for the Little Big Man to continue.

‘You know that clearing next to the river, about five hundred yards from here?’

The commander nodded.

‘Good,’ continued Tad. ‘We would like you to get your chaps to place one thousand archers’ dummies there, placed in ranks of fifty, right across the clearing.’

Once again, the two Fair-Folk showed visible signs of surprise.

‘May I ask why?’ enquired Ammon.

‘Demonstration,’ said Nathaniel abruptly. ‘Then we talk.’

Ammon stood up. ‘I shall do as you have asked. But I must warn you; this had better be worth it. I am not here to be joshed with.’

The commander and the mage left the tent.

As they reached the door Nathaniel

called out. ‘Commander.’

Ammon turned to face him. ‘Yes, Marine.’

‘Thank you for the coffee. We are genuinely in your debt; it was very kind of you.’

The commander bowed his acceptance of the compliment and swept from the tent.

Tad turned to Nathaniel, a strict expression on his face. ‘I must warn you,’ he said. ‘I am not here to be joshed with.’

Both men burst out laughing.

Nathaniel was impressed. True to his word, Ammon had commanded his people to work through the night, and when the sun rose; it did so on a field of a thousand archers' dummies, positioned in neat ranks of one hundred.

He turned to the small group of armed men behind him. 'Right, guys,' he said. 'Just as we discussed before. Jackson, Peters, Cameron, and Smith. I want you to move a hundred yards closer to the targets. Remember, we're looking to show firepower here, so I want you on full automatic fire, change magazines quickly, and sweep from side to side.

Vickers and Bren teams, on my mark, same thing. We'll start with a mortar round. I have already set the tube up and it should be bang on the target, and then fire another two at will. Right, everyone to their marks.'

Then the Marine and Tad walked over to Commander Ammon and the small group of Fair-Folk that were seated under a tented pavilion. The two humans sat on the right hand of the commander in seats provided.

'Well, Commander,' said Nathaniel. 'Time for the demonstration.'

Ammon nodded. The expression on his bland features hinted at condescension as he waited for Nathaniel and his humans to perform their parlor trick.

The Forever Man drew in a little power and used it to project his voice to his people. Seth tilted his head in

interest as he noted the human's subtle use of the pulse light.

'Mortar crew,' said Nathanial. 'First round, fire.'

Contrary to popular belief, perpetuated by Hollywood, a mortar does not make a polite pop when fired. In reality, it discharges with a solid thump that can be felt in one's gut, then it screams through the air with a sound like a banshee, and ends with a brain-jarring explosion that shakes the ground and vibrates your brain about in your skull.

And that is exactly what happened, the high explosive mortar round exploded, blowing down at least a hundred of the dummies, smashing them to pieces as it did so.

But there was no time for the Fair-Folk to react as Nathaniel immediately ordered his Thompsons and Sten guns to open up. The hand-held submachine guns spat out steel-jacketed lead rounds at a combined rate of over twenty rounds a second, chewing into the remaining dummies.

Then the heavy machine guns opened up with a sound like a giant tearing a thousand telephone books in half. Close to forty rounds a second swept across the target area as another mortar round exploded and then another.

In less than one full minute, over two thousand steel-jacketed rounds and three high explosive mortar bombs had reduced the ranks of archer's dummies to mere smoking piles of rags and kindling.

Nathaniel turned to Commander Ammon of the Fair-Folk.

'Demonstration over. Time to talk.'

Ammon shook his head in disbelief. 'What magik is that?' he asked as he looked to Seth for some input.

Seth Hil-Nu shrugged. 'I could detect no magiks,' he said. 'Only the small amount that the Marine used to hail his warriors.'

'They are pre-pulse human weapons,' said Nathaniel. 'And we have many more of them. Enough to destroy the Annihilators.' He pulled a Colt 45 out of his pocket and showed it to Ammon. 'This is called a semi-auto pistol.' The Marine ejected the magazine and then racked the slide, popping out the round that was in the chamber. He handed the 45 APC cartridge to the commander. 'This is what makes the pistol work. However, once you have used it you cannot use it again. It is spent. We have a limited number of these, so we need to engineer a decisive battle where we can destroy the Annihilators in one fell swoop.'

Nathaniel waited for Ammon to reply but it was obvious that he would have to give him and Seth some more time to process what had just happened. The shock of witnessing the destructive capabilities of modern firepower had overwhelmed the Fair-Folk observers and they all needed some time to adjust their thinking.

Seth spoke first. 'Before we came here, leaving our former home, I traveled through time and space to observe the humans in order to ascertain whether your land would be a viable place for us to relocate. During those travels I saw, first hand, the effect of massed weapons such as these. It was horrific. I would like to know how many you have.'

'Enough,' answered Nathaniel.

'Would you care to be more specific?'

'No,' said the Marine. 'And anyway,

specifics would be meaningless.'

'What would stop you turning these weapons on us?' asked Ammon.

'That is not our intention,' answered Nathaniel. 'It is our goal to ally ourselves with you, and together we will defeat and eliminate the Annihilators.'

'But what about after that?' insisted Ammon.

'After that is another time,' said Nathaniel. 'But I can assure you that we would not simply attack you. I believe that a peaceful solution can be reached between us. Personally, I have had enough of battle. I would love to rule over a people at peace. To look to the future with happiness as opposed to trepidation.'

'Then so be it,' said Ammon. 'We are at your disposal, Marine Sergeant. What do you suggest?'

So, Nathaniel told the commander.

The plan was a simple one, but it did involve a massive coordination of troop movements and a great deal of fairly precise timing.

The Marine proposed that the Fair-Folk gathered their entire army and advanced on a massive front towards the Annihilators, moving slowly but methodically, setting up fortified stockades each night and advancing carefully and in strength. Nathaniel also promised the Fair-Folk a large contingent of air support in the form of three thousand Vandal flyers. The stockades, the air power, and the large numbers of Orcs, goblins, and trolls would make them an unattractive target for the Annihilators.

While they were doing this, the humans would perform a series of lightning strikes against the Roaches, hitting them hard and then withdrawing back behind the wall, leaving a vacuum behind them as they retreated. If the Annihilators did attack the humans then Nathaniel would ensure that they would fall back in seeming disarray, simulating a desperate retreat.

It was the Marine's thought that the Annihilator leadership would assume that the humans were on their last legs, and by attacking them in force, they would be able to send them scurrying back beyond the wall to lick their wounds. And then the Annihilators would be able to turn their full attention to defeating the Fair-Folk.

It would be at this point, when the Annihilator army was situated close to the wall, that the Fair-Folk would advance through a series of forced marches thereby pinning the Roach army between the wall and the entire Fair-Folk army.

Then, Nathaniel would unleash his pre-pulse weapons, and in a combined assault from both humans and Fair-Folk, they would utterly destroy their shared foe.

Ammon asked if he could have some time with his advisors and Nathaniel agreed, saying that he and Tad would be in his tent enjoying another mug of coffee.

The two humans had just finished their second mug of coffee when Ammon and Seth arrived and asked permission to enter the tent. Tad stood and ushered them in.

‘It shall be done,’ said Ammon. ‘We will start to consolidate our troops tomorrow morning. It will take us seven days to completely mobilize all of our forces and another ten to position them into the correct areas. We shall begin our advance eighteen days hence.’

Donald Rathbone lived alone. Very alone. In fact, Donald had not interacted with another human being for almost twelve years. In less confused times he would have been considered a hermit. Or perhaps a religious aesthete, living a life of austerity and contemplation.

As it happened, Donald was none of these things. What Donald was, was completely insane. Twenty years ago, after the pulse and on seeing his first Orcs and goblins, Donald had suffered a complete mental break from reality.

This was due to the fact that he knew that Orcs and goblins did not exist. However, he was patently seeing them. Ipso facto—he must be insane. And, as an insane person, he deduced that he would no longer be safe in a normal, sane, society.

So, he went to live in the deepest woods, surviving off the land and sleeping in an old grotto dressed in the barest remnants of clothing that had survived his self-enforced banishment.

This morning, Donald rose with the sparrows, drank deeply from the brook that babbled past his grotto and then went in search of food. As per usual, he collected up a handful of grubs and the odd root. Then, seeing a bird nest high in an oak tree, he decided to climb to the top in order to check if the nest contained any eggs.

Slowly, testing each branch before he climbed on to it, he made his way to the uppermost boughs of the tree. He reached the branch that the nest was on and peered in. Empty.

Donald sighed philosophically and looked over the surrounding treetops to the horizon beyond the forest.

And as far as he could see, stretching from the west to the east, were thousands upon thousands of marching Orcs, goblins, and trolls. Above them flew hundreds of bat-like people, large leathern wings keeping them aloft.

The old man chuckled to himself. What a sight that would be if it actually existed, he thought.

He climbed carefully back down the oak tree. On the way down, he came across a large tree-snail.

He put it in his food bag to eat later.

Greg was nineteen years old and this was his first command. When he had told his parents and his sister about being chosen, they had been inordinately proud. As had his girlfriend, Mandy. In fact, she had been so impressed that Greg finally got to get to third base … and beyond.

The Little Big Man himself had picked this team, as he had the forty-nine other teams. There were twenty soldiers per team, young, fit, and agile. All were mounted and proficient with bow and sword.

Their mission was simplicity itself; find the Roaches, attack, hit hard and run. That was it.

But even the best laid plans of mice and men go astray.

It had taken a week to find a Roach patrol and Greg had positioned his men with great care.

He had left two guarding the houses, situated in a small fold in the land about half a mile from the Roach camp. Then he had followed the natural fold to the camp, setting up an ambush halfway down. Ten of his men lining the sides of the small valley. Finally, he and the final seven had crept up on the camp itself.

The plan was to attack, retreat and then ambush the pursuers, knocking more of them out before all running to the horses and then getting the hell out of Dodge.

His second-in-command, Tommy Halse, was less than happy.

'Greg,' he whispered as they lay under cover outside the Roach camp. 'I'm worried that we're overcomplicating things. Can't we just hit them and run. After all, that's what we're meant to do. Straight forward and simple. That's what The Little Big Man told us. Hit and run.'

'Listen, Tommy,' answered Greg, an

expression of superiority etched across his face. 'You may be happy to do the bare minimum, but I'm looking to do more. That's why I was chosen as a commander and not you. I go the extra yard. You don't. So why don't you just shut it and do as you're told. Or are you chicken?'

Tommy shook his head. 'Of course not,' he denied. 'That's unfair.'

'Well then,' continued Greg. 'On my command, we attack.'

The word went down the line, whispered from one man's mouth to the next man's ear. The tension grew as tight as new tuned piano wire as the men waited for Greg's command.

Finally, the young man rose to his feet, bow already drawn. 'Fire' he yelled, and he unleashed his arrow. It was a great shot, hitting one of the Roach guards in the middle of his chest and punching through him, knocking him to the floor.

The rest of the men sprang up and unleashed their arrows. The sound of steel smashing through armored carapaces rang out. Roaches dropped, squealing to the ground.

One of the insectoid warriors fell into the camp fire and Greg was astounded to see that it immediately burst into flame. That must have been partly why the fire storm happened, he thought to himself, the Roaches are flammable. I must remember to tell The Little Big Man.

Greg was surprised at how swiftly the Roaches rallied, some of them drawing their bows and firing back while others formed up into ranks.

'Let's go,' he shouted to his men. 'Withdraw.'

He sprinted off in the direction of the ambush that he had laid across the small valley, followed by his men.

But their retreat did not go as smoothly as planned, due to the fact that the Annihilators had rallied their forces so quickly. Every twenty or thirty paces, Greg and his men had to turn and fight, loosing more arrows at their pursuers and cutting down the odd Roach that got close enough to actually engage in hand-to-hand combat.

By the time that Greg's small group got to the ambush point they were close to exhaustion, feet dragging as they barely managed to keep ahead of the enemy. In fact, they were so close that the ambushers were unable to unleash their bows as they were afraid to hit their own compatriots. So, instead, they simply charged and took on the Annihilators hand-to-hand.

The humans fought with desperation, drawing on reserves of energy that they didn't even know that they had, their youthful energy and speed making up for their lack of combat experience.

Finally, they had dispatched all of their pursuers, although they had lost four of their own.

'We did it,' panted Greg as he surveyed the fallen Roaches about him.

'Looks like we did,' admitted Tommy. 'Why are there so few of them?'

'What do you mean?' asked Greg.

'Look,' said Tommy. 'I thought that

there were more of them. There's only ten or so bodies.'

'It just looked like there were more,' said Greg. 'They're very good fighters. We did well. You did well.' He patted Tommy on the back, magnanimous in his victory.

The exhausted survivors staggered back down the valley to their horses.

Greg was really looking forward to getting home. He would be modest when he told all of his victory. Praising his men while still ensuring that all knew of his plan.

He imagined The Little Big Man's approbation and admiration as he told all that Greg, instead of running, had destroyed an entire unit of Roaches. Perhaps he would even be introduced to the king. The Forever Man.

He was jerked out of his reverie by Tommy's sharp retort.

'The horses,' he said. 'What the …'

Greg peered into the darkness. 'They're lying down,' he said to Tommy.

‘No, they’re not,’ snapped Tommy. ‘They’re all dead.’

As he spoke, at least fifty Roach warriors stepped out from the trees, surrounding the small group of humans.

‘They must have flanked us while we were fighting the others in that ambush of yours,’ continued Tommy. He grabbed Greg by his shirt front. ‘Well done, you arrogant ass,’ he said. ‘You’ve killed us all.’

And the Annihilators fell upon them, ululating and screeching as they hacked them to shreds.

'We've lost eight commando groups in the last two days,' said Tad. 'All totally wiped out. That's one hundred and sixty men. We have to do something about it. It can't go on like this. I suggest that we increase the size of the commando groups, maybe one hundred. Venture out in strength. Also, the ratio of young inexperienced men is far too high. I think that we need to put at least thirty older more experienced warriors in each enlarged group. A captain or lieutenant in charge, instead of some newbie. What do you think?'

Nathaniel stood on the battlements of the wall and stared out across the open land and into enemy held territory. 'Have the Fair-Folk engaged the Roaches yet?' he asked, ignoring Tad's question completely.

'Nothing major,' answered Tad. 'A

few minor scuffles, but on the whole, they seem to be pushing the Annihilators our way.'

'So,' continued the Marine. 'All seems to be going according to plan. Would you agree?'

'On the whole, yes,' agreed Tad.

'So why do you want to put it all at risk by changing the plan?'

'I don't want to change the plan, per se,' argued Tad. 'I simply want to bolster the commando groups. One hundred and sixty lives are too many.'

'Acceptable losses,' said Nathaniel.

'No losses are acceptable,' argued Tad. 'At least let me put some experienced men in charge of each group.'

Nathaniel shook his head. 'Young men fight hard and take risks. Age and experience brings with it a certain reticence. We want the Annihilators to perceive our random attacks as a final act of desperation. Throwing our young men in their path in a futile ability to slow them down as they approach our final defenses.'

'So,' said Tad. 'What you are saying is that we need to take casualties. It's part of your plan.'

'Regrettably, yes,' sighed Nathaniel.

'That's cold,' said Tad. That's really cold. I don't think that I can agree to that.'

The Forever Man turned and looked at Tad. His eyes bored into him, blazing like fire-lit emeralds. A frisson of fear rippled through the Little Big Man. He felt like a domesticated dog that has just been confronted by a full-grown wolf for the first time. A disturbing mix of fear and respect and a need to please.

'I never told you to agree with it,' said The Forever Man. 'I have simply told you to do it.'

Tad bowed slightly. 'And so it shall be done, my king,' he said. 'Even though it wounds my very soul to do so.'

The Little Big Man turned on his heel and walked away, leaving Nathaniel alone on the wall.

'It wounds me too,' whispered Nathaniel. 'And I shall have to live with it forever.'

In the next week they lost another ten score warriors. Two hundred young men, not yet out of their teens.

And the Annihilator advance continued across the front, heading for the killing ground in front of the wall.

Ammon stared at the Vandal standing in front of him. The Fair-Folk commander made no attempt to hide the distaste that he felt towards the scrawny bat-like creature with its huge leathern wings, sharp teeth, and skinny bow legs. However, although he detested the creatures on a personal basis, he could not argue as to the fact that access to aerial observation, combined with the ability to bombard the enemy and to negate the threat of their flying Yari, must surely give one a marked advantage when it came to tactics.

However, Ammon had yet to figure out how to change his customary tactics that had always worked so well against the Elven hive-creatures that he had battled so successfully on his home planet.

Grim-son stood at semi-attention,

deliberately allowing himself to slouch to one side and assuming a vacant expression simply to antagonize the little gray thing in front of him.

He couldn't quite figure out why, but the moment that the Vandal Wing Commander had been introduced to the Fair-Folk he had found that he was overwhelmed by an instant and intense feeling of dislike. However, King Nathaniel had asked him and his fellow flyers to assist the rubber heads and he had agreed. He missed working with the humans. He missed their innate sense of humor and their unconscious kindness as well as their bravery and skills in battle. They were good friends and even better allies.

On the other end of the scale were the Fair-Folk. When it came to making military decisions, Grim-son found them to be tactically naïve and totally without imagination. Their standard battle tactic was to simply march massed ranks of heavily armed infantry, supported by massive trolls, straight down the enemy's throat. Goblin archers were used as simply covering fire or to soften up the enemy before a charge.

'So, you are sure on your numbers?' asked Ammon again.

Grim-son nodded. Three thousand Annihilator foot warriors and less than five hundred flying Yari. They are encamped about five miles away, behind the mountain at the end of the valley.

'Have they set sentries?'

'Some,' affirmed Grim-son. 'But they are overconfident. They do not fear attack from you and your people. Your lack of aggression has lulled them into a feeling of security. At the moment, the few sentries that they do have are on the northern side of the camp, about a mile out. Long-range scouts guarding against human attackers.'

Ammon sat back in his chair and thought for a while. He had no real desire to engage with the Annihilators, but he was now inextricably linked to King Nathaniel's plan. If he did not keep some sort of pressure on the Annihilators, ensuring that they kept moving north towards the retreating humans, then there was every chance that they would turn on his advancing troops. He shuddered to think what fifty thousand plus Annihilator warriors might do to his Orcs and goblins. They were a warrior class that fought with consummate skill and passion, as opposed to the Orcs that were bred more for following orders and fighting solidly and stoically against a less motivated enemy. Their shortcomings had already been greatly exposed by the humans in the few major skirmishes that they had ever had with them. Ammon was the first to admit that they had been outfought and outmaneuvered every time.

It was only the scarcity of human Free State numbers that had prevented them from actually attacking the Fair-Folk in an aggressive way.

He stood up, decision made. He had almost fifty thousand Orcs and goblins under his direct control, so attacking a mere three thousand Annihilators should not pose any great threat. And a victory would be good for everyone's morale. Plus, it would show that ghastly, self-important Forever Man that the Fair-Folk were doing their share of the work.

'We will attack,' he told Grim-son. 'Ready your flyers and tell them to keep the Yari off our backs.'

Grim-son nodded. 'Would you like us to bombard them? We have some naphtha flasks.'

'No,' said Ammon. 'Just do as I have already asked. Keep the Yari at bay.'

The Vandal Wing Commander bowed, bending far lower than was necessary as he subtly mocked the Fair-Folk leader. 'So be it,' he said as he left and headed back to his squadron.

Ammon pulled in a little of the power provided by the life light and he pulsed Seth Hil-Nu.

Minutes later the paramount mage arrived. 'You called.'

'Greetings, mage,' replied Ammon. 'The Vandal scouts have found an encampment of Annihilators at the end of the valley some five miles from us. Three thousand strong. I have decided to attack. The bat creatures will keep the Yari off our backs and we shall simply overwhelm the Roaches with superior numbers. Goblin archers to the fore, arrow storm then a running charge from the Orcs. I propose setting them in fifty ranks of one thousand. Finish this whole thing as quickly as possible. Can you and the other mages help?'

'Certainly, Commander,' assured Seth. 'We can provide support in the form of fireballs and lightning, but perhaps we should refrain.'

'Why?' enquired Ammon.

'With such overwhelming odds, I doubt whether mage support would be required, and I am afraid that it might attract unnecessary attention. Thunderbolts and fireballs can be seen and heard from great distances away. The last thing that we need is to attract unwanted attention from another larger force of Annihilators.'

‘True, my friend,’ agreed Ammon. ‘Well said. Tell your men to refrain from using magiks unless absolutely necessary. Now go forth and inform the Orc sergeants to prepare to move out, battle formations in ranks of one thousand.’

‘So be it,’ said Seth as he bowed low. Unlike Grim-son, there was no hint of mockery in his obeisance.

Ammon sat in his chair and prepared himself for the upcoming battle. It had been many years since he had last been personally involved in anything larger than a scuffle, and he went over the plan in his mind. It wasn’t difficult; he would simply do what he had always done. Victory was inevitable.

Outside his tent waited four Orcs who were spanned to a two-wheel cart like oxen. Seth was already in the buggy.

Not for the first time, Ammon wished that they could have found some way to convince horses to work with the Fair-Folk or the Orcs. Still, Orc power was far preferable to walking and a good Orc could travel as far as, although not as fast as, a horse.

With his fifty thousand troops in the vanguard, Commander Ammon set off to do battle against the three thousand Annihilators.

The massed Orcs kept their formations well, even over the rough ground that they had to cover. The trip in the buggy was not too onerous, although Ammon did have to have some stern words with the Orcs when they lurched a little over the rougher parts of the track.

Then they breasted a rise and got their first view of the Annihilator camp. Grimson had been correct; there were no more than three thousand of the insectoid creatures. But this was the first time that Ammon had actually seen an Annihilator and he was unprepared for the sight. With their gaudy armor and bladed appendages, they were a truly formidable sight, and the Fair-Folk commander felt a flutter of nervous fear ripple through him.

The Annihilators reacted immediately

as they caught sight of the massed ranks of Orcs approaching. Smoothly, and without any signs of panic, the Annihilators formed up, facing the Orc army.

Ammon turned to Seth. 'Mage, sound the attack. Orcs to form up in ranks twenty-five deep and two thousand wide. Approach at a slow trot.'

The mage drew in power and used it to enhance his voice. His order to advance at a trot boomed across the valley, and the ground shook as over fifty thousand feet struck the earth in time.

Ammon waited for the Orcs to get closer, and when they were five hundred yards from the enemy, he relayed his next order to Seth.

'Archers, fire,'

The order was relayed, and the sky darkened as thousands of arrows were unleashed towards the enemy, momentarily blocking out the sun.

'Orcs, lock shields.'

The order to lock shields echoed

across the valley and there was a resounding crash as fifty thousand steel edged shields banged up tight against each other.

'Now, charge,' commanded Ammon.

'Charge!' relayed Seth and the horde broke into a sprint heading towards the three thousand Annihilators.

Ammon nodded to himself as the pageant of war unfolded in front of him. The outcome would be swift and inevitable. The Annihilators would undoubtedly fight back with great skill and valor, but they would simply be overwhelmed by the charge. Fifty thousand against three thousand was an advantage that was simply impossible to overcome.

But as the Orcs charged the Annihilators, instead of bracing for the impact, the Roaches split their forces in half and, running at an unbelievable speed, they went left and right, angling backwards as they did so.

At the same time, hundreds of Yari launched themselves into the air and headed towards the charging Orcs.

But Grim-son and his Vandals had been waiting for this and they came screaming out of the sun and slammed into the Yari, shooting their crossbows as they engaged in a wheeling, turning aerial dogfight.

The Annihilators continued to angle away from the Orc charge, and by the time the Orcs had arrived at the area where they had expected to make contact with the enemy, there was no one there and the charge began to lose its impetus.

The Annihilators, who had now completely outflanked the Orcs on both left and right, stopped running, turned and threw themselves at the Fair-Folk army, hitting them from the sides and thereby negating the shield wall.

The ordered ranks of Orcs immediately broke down into a disorganized mêlée as the Roach warriors slashed and cut their way deep into the massed formation.

'What are they doing?' yelled

Ammon. 'Tell the Orcs to wheel. Quickly.'

'Orcs, wheel left and right,' relayed Seth.

'Tell the goblins to fire at the enemy,' added Ammon in a panic. 'Now, do it now.'

'Archers, fire at will,' communicated Seth.

Arrows rained down on the battling warriors striking Orc and Roach alike. Orcs stumbled over each other as they tried to wheel whilst the Annihilators hacked and cut at them.

Finally, every semblance of order fell apart and the battle turned into a primal struggle to kill or be killed. And Commander Ammon could do little more than simply watch it unfold.

As it happened, the Fair-Folk commander was correct in his initial assumption that three thousand cannot beat fifty thousand. As the battle wore on, the sheer weight of Orc numbers brought the Annihilators to heel, wearing them out, and eventually, dispatching every last one of them.

The victory cost Commander Ammon almost twenty thousand troops. Eighteen thousand Orcs and two thousand goblin archers. A kill ratio of around eight-to-one against him. He shuddered to think what would happen if there had been five or six thousand Annihilators, because if truth be told, he probably would have still attacked, believing that a ten to one advantage would be sufficient. And then he might have lost.

This one relatively small skirmish had convinced Ammon that he had made the correct decision when he ordered the Fair-Folk to remain out of the Human-Annihilator battles as much as possible.

It also proved something else. According to his intelligence reports, the human warriors were achieving a kill ratio against the Roaches of around five to one in the human's favor. That meant, that if they ever took it into their heads to gamble everything on an all-out push against the Fair-Folk, it would be a close-run thing, even though the Fair-Folk grossly outnumbered them. And that fact got

Commander Ammon to start on some serious thinking.

Nathaniel's plan was working. Slowly and inexorably the Annihilators were being drawn closer, hunting down the small bands of human raiders and subtly avoiding any major confrontation with the hundreds of thousands of Orcs and goblins driving north.

The Roach plan was obvious, they would overcome the dwindling and desperate human opposition, consolidate at the wall, and then turn all of their attention to the approaching Fair-Folk army.

It was a good plan, tactically sound. It's only negative was that it was exactly what Nathaniel wanted them to do. But they had no way of knowing that.

Tad had taken to avoiding the Marine, speaking to him only when necessary.

Since the Little Big Man had first brought it up that he believed the youthful commando groups were taking unnecessary losses and Nathaniel had overruled him, Tad had become very uncommunicative. He did all that he was told and more, he simply spent as little time with the Marine as possible.

Nathaniel decided that he had to do something about the state of affairs and he sent for Tad, asking him to meet him on the wall.

The Little Big Man arrived, saluted, and then stood at ease, waiting.

'So formal, my friend?' asked Nathaniel.

'I live but to serve, sire,' answered Tad.

'Oh, cut it out,' replied Nathaniel. 'Get off your high horse and stop acting like an ass. What's your problem?'

Tad said nothing.

'Come on,' insisted Nathaniel. 'Speak freely.'

‘We have now lost over a thousand young men on our commando raids,’ said Tad.

‘So?’ replied Nathaniel.

‘So,’ said Tad. ‘We could have avoided that.’

‘We have already discussed this.’

‘No, we haven’t,’ said Tad. ‘I brought it up and you ignored me. Because of us, innocents are dying.’

‘There are no innocents in war,’ snapped Nathaniel.

‘Oh, don’t be so glib,’ said Tad. ‘We’re not talking in sound bites here. This is reality. Kids are going out, they’re not experienced enough, and their inexperience is getting them killed.’

‘They are not kids,’ said Nathaniel. ‘They are over sixteen. Most are around nineteen. The average age of the combat soldier in Vietnam was nineteen. In the American War of Independence, boys as young as fifteen fought. There are no innocents. There are no children. There are only soldiers and I am their commander. I am their leader. I am their king and they shall do as I command. As will you.'

There was an uncomfortable silence as both men glowered at each other.

Finally, Tad spoke. And when he did so his face showed the depth of his emotion. 'You're right,' he said. His voice barely above a whisper. 'I know that it has to be done, it's just that I can't handle it. Watching those youngsters go out every day, full of thoughts of glory and duty and then returning all bloodied and dying and cut to pieces. I simply don't think that I can handle it anymore. So, I blame you, it's easier.'

Nathaniel put his hand on his friend's shoulder. 'That's fine,' he said. 'I don't mind accepting the blame; after all, it was my order. But don't let the boys see your despair. If they are going to die let them die with honor. With glory. Rather than in fear. Give them something to die for, and in doing so you may help them to actually live longer.'

Tad nodded. ‘I will try.’

‘Good,’ said Nathaniel. ‘It won’t be for much longer. Days. No more.’

Tad left the wall, forcing his head high as he went to motivate the next group of commandos leaving on their raid.

The Annihilator army had been massing for the last four days, meeting at a site three miles from the wall. Nathaniel had sent word, via Vandal flyers, to Commander Ammon, urging him to speed up his advance. The Annihilators will attack at any moment, he had said. Your presence is imperative. Together we shall crush them, the wall shall be the anvil and you shall be the hammer.

Ammon had heeded the call and now he had over five hundred thousand Orcs and goblins positioned in a semi-circle a mile away from the Annihilator camp.

The sun rose at five forty-two the next morning. The sky was clear, and a cold wind blew from the south east. The ground was covered with a thin blanket of snow. White, crystalline, and clean. A wedding dress laid out for a virgin bride. Or maybe a linen shroud, pure and unsullied, readied to wrap the body of a loved one.

And before the wall, standing in ordered ranks, stood over sixty thousand Annihilators. Behind them were ten thousand flying Yari, ready to take to the air and rain steel death down on the wall.

Nathaniel stood next to Tad, and Orc Sergeant Kob, looking out over the enemy.

'End game,' he said.

Tad nodded. 'I know that this may be a little too late to ask, but do you think that we have enough firepower to win this thing?'

The Marine shrugged. 'All depends. If we can keep them packed together enough for the machine guns to have a real effect. If enough Vandals can get through the Yari cover to drop the grenades and the fire bombs. If the rubber heads ensure that their goblins put a serious quantity of arrows into the air. If, if, if. Well, yes, maybe. Who knows?'

Tad laughed. 'Good. I'm glad that you

cleared that up. I was confused before.'

Nathaniel joined in with his laughter. 'You know what it's like,' he said. 'Every plan goes to crap the moment the battle starts. But, let me put it this way—I wouldn't have put so much at risk, lost so many lives, and spent so long getting to this point if I didn't truly believe that we had a good chance of pulling it off.'

Tad nodded. 'Well, that's good enough for me.'

Kob grunted. 'Battle is battle. Plans are only a suggestion that lasts until the sound of the first clash of blades.'

'Very philosophical,' said Tad, sarcastically.

Kob did not deign to answer.

The sun rose above the trees, a huge crimson orb that painted the virgin snow with a wash of red, a forerunner of the blood that would soak the earth ere the day was over.

The Annihilators started to rub their bladed forearms together, producing a high-pitched screech.

‘Time to sing, boys,’ shouted Tad as he lifted his voice, singing in a clear tenor. The humans joined in as one.

Mine eyes have seen the glory of the coming of the Lord;

He is trampling out the vintage where the grapes of wrath are stored;

He hath loosed the fateful lightning of His terrible swift sword:

His truth is marching on.

Ten thousand Yari took to the wing, rising up into the clear morning sky. As did the three thousand Vandal fighters that had been hiding in the treetops. The Yari drove hard, trying to get enough height to drop their steel darts. But, within seconds the Vandals were on to them, firing their crossbows and throwing their nets to entangle the enemy and drive them back to earth.

With an ear-shattering shriek, the Annihilators started forward, fanning out as they ran, ladders at the ready.

Nathaniel had placed the four Vickers guns one hundred yards apart on the top of the wall.

The six Bren guns had been situated outside the wall, secreted in the forest to the right and left of the Annihilator charge. With the Bren guns, hidden in the forest, were two thousand cavalry, also split into two teams divided to the left and right of the Roach charge. Out of those two teams, sixty were armed with Thompson and Sten submachine guns and Colt 45s.

The four mortars were placed well back from the wall, as there was no reason for them to be exposed and Nathaniel had already sighted them in, ready to fire at his command.

On the top of the wall he also had ten men armed with the submachine guns and Colts, including the one 45 that he had kept for himself, tucked into his belt.

'When are we going to fire?' asked Tad.

'Not yet,' answered Nathaniel. 'They're still too spread out. We need

Ammon to start to close the circle. Bunch them up. Until that happens, we just have to push them back off the wall the old-fashioned way.'

The Marine concentrated and pulsed a message to Seth, the Fair-Folk mage, urging him to move the Orcs forward to force the Annihilator ranks together, thus providing a denser target area. The mage pulsed back that he would relay the message.

By this time, the charging Annihilators were almost at the wall.

'Archers!' shouted Nathaniel. 'Fire at will.'

A deluge of cloth-yard shafts rained down on the front rows of the Annihilators, smashing through their exoskeletons and driving hundreds to the ground. But the next row picked up the ladders and ran over their fallen comrades.

Over one hundred ladders were thrown up against the walls and the Roaches swarmed up to be met with a frantic human defense. The humans all knew that this was the last battle, win or lose, and they were literally throwing themselves at the enemy.

Such was the fervor of the human defense that the ladders were cleared from the wall and the initial rows of attackers dispatched within a few minutes.

But the Annihilators were made of stern stuff, and the next ranks picked up the ladders and resumed the attack. The humans fought back desperately with swords and axe and dagger. Nathaniel had given strict orders that no firearms could be used until he had given his express order as he did not want to show his hand too early.

Again, the Roaches were repelled and again they gathered for the next attack.

Nathaniel pulsed Seth again. ‘Listen,’ he urged. ‘We need some help here. Get your archers to rake the back ranks with arrows, take some of the heat off us. And then tighten the circle, for God’s sake. I need the Roaches to be packed together to get the full effect of my ordnance.’

Once again, Seth pulsed back that he

would relay the message.

A ladder was thrown against the wall at Nathaniel's feet, and he waited for the first Roach to appear at the top before he brained it with his axe and sent it plummeting backwards, taking three others with it as it fell. Then the Marine put his foot against the top of the ladder and pushed hard, thrusting it back into the massed ranks of enemy warriors.

All along the wall similar resistance was occurring, and for the first time, the Annihilators retreated in good order to properly regroup. As it happened, the last assault had sorely tested the human resistance, pushing it to its limit. The men were tired beyond belief after throwing back three consecutive and concentrated attacks. It was lucky, however, that the Annihilators were as exhausted, and had to regroup.

'Seth!' pulsed Nathaniel. 'Now. Advance, now.'

'What are they doing?' asked Tad. 'Where are the Orcs? Where is the goblin arrow storm? What the hell is going on?'

Nathaniel peered over the ranks of the Annihilators and looked at the distant masses of Orcs. He shook his head. 'They're doing nothing,' he said.

Kob pointed. 'Look, I think that they are starting to move.'

'Well, if they are, they are doing it so slowly as to make no difference,' snapped Nathaniel.

'What now?' asked Tad. 'Our boys can't take much more of this.'

Nathaniel glanced up, the sky was still full of cartwheeling, spinning, and falling bodies as the Yari and the Vandals continued their fight. On the ground, the Annihilators were almost back into rank formation and it would be a mere few minutes before the next charge. The Marine took a deep breath and made his decision.

First, he contacted the teenager that was sitting with the ground support Vandals, waiting for Nathaniel's command.

'Fly,' he pulsed. 'Grenade and bomb attack as soon as possible. Watch out for bogies above, there is still a strong Yari presence but that can't be helped. Do what you can.'

'Next, he pulsed the leaders of the cavalry directly, using a psychic link that he had established earlier. 'Cavalry. Slight change of plan. On my command I want you to charge the enemy flanks. Come in on a broad front. We need to compact them together as much as possible. Godspeed, gentlemen, we shall meet afterwards for a drink. They'll be on me.'

Finally, he pulsed his machine gunners and mortar operators. 'On my command, a fireball in the air, you rain down fire. Good hunting, chaps.'

Then Nathaniel turned to Tad and held out his hand. The Little Big Man shook it.

'To the end, my friend,' said Nathaniel.

'To the end,' returned Tad.

Then they stood silent for a moment,

waiting for the Annihilators to commence their charge. As soon as they did, Nathaniel pulled in power to enhance the volume of his voice.

'Charge!' The command echoed across the battlefield like a crash of thunder.

Two thousand horses came galloping out of the forest in an avalanche of steel and fury. As they closed, the men with the submachine guns opened up. The effect was instantaneous and the Annihilators reacted with shocked panic as the steel-covered lead bullets chewed into them, driving hundreds of warriors back in a welter of blood and chips of carapace.

As the massed Annihilators bunched together, forced by the charging cavalry, Nathaniel pulsed his mortar crew.

'Fire one round each.'

There was a solid thud as the four mortars threw their explosive payload high into the air. Then the whistling cacophony of the shells plunging to earth followed by four massive explosions. The HE rounds landed near the rear of the Annihilator ranks, in the exact position that Nathaniel wanted them to. Body parts and earth were tossed into the air like leaves in an autumn wind.

'Fire again,' pulsed Nathaniel. 'And then fire at will.'

The Annihilators rushed at the wall, crushing each other together as they pushed forward in an attempt to escape the explosions that were marching across their rear ranks.

Just before they were close enough to throw their scaling ladders up against the wall, Nathaniel drew in power, formed a massive orange ball of fire above his head, and then punched it into the sky.

It arced overhead like a meteor, blazing and crackling for all to see.

Ten machine guns opened up as one, pouring a torrent of hot lead slugs into the massed Annihilators. Moving methodically from side to side as they scythed the enemy down in a wave of destruction.

The men on the wall cocked their

submachine guns and fired down into the Roaches with short accurate bursts, driving them back into the mortar explosions and machine gun fire.

And then the Vandal ground support flyers appeared over the treetops, coming in at just over one hundred feet. They dropped their Mills Grenades and Naphthalene bombs as they flew past. Shrapnel tore into the packed enemy and fire stuck to them as they exploded into flame.

The orgy of destruction lasted for less than five full minutes. In that short space of time over sixty thousand rounds of ammunition were expended and hundreds of explosive bombs and grenades.

In those terrifying unholy three hundred seconds, over thirty thousand living beings had been extinguished.

Alien medieval-era warriors torn to shreds by modern weaponry in human hands.

Then Nathaniel gave the command to open the gates in the wall and the humans poured out, charging into the dazed and broken Annihilator warriors. The Forever Man was with them.

The twenty thousand Annihilator survivors fought back with utter desperation, looking to destroy as many humans as possible before they were dispatched. Hoping desperately to turn the tide and take the wall before the Fair-Folk army moved on them.

The battle had degenerated into hundreds of separate skirmishes as small groups of warriors clashed and fought to the death. Both humans and Annihilators were still dying in the thousands.

Tad, Kob, and Nathaniel cut through the center of the massive mêlée. The Orc and the Little Big Man supporting the Marine as he struggled to reach the Annihilator leader, deducing from the last time he beat a Supreme Warrior that it would take the wind out of the Annihilator sails if he killed the leader.

Akimiri Hijiti, the undisputed Hatomoto, or Supreme Warrior of the

Annihilators saw The Forever Man hacking his way through the press of fighting warriors in an attempt to meet him. The Supreme Warrior yelled out to his men.

'Clear the way for the human Hatomoto,' he shouted as he strode towards Nathaniel. 'He is mine.'

As they approached each other the Annihilator leader called out to the Marine. 'At last we meet,' he said. 'It will be my greatest honor to take your life in mortal combat.'

'In your dreams,' quipped the Marine.

And he pulled the Colt 45 from his belt, aimed, and pulled the trigger, emptying the entire magazine into the Annihilator's chest.

Akimiri Hijiti, the undisputed Hatomoto, or Supreme Warrior of the Annihilators fell backwards, dead before he reached the ground, his chest a mass of bloody holes.

'Sorry, Mister Supreme Warrior dude,' said Nathaniel. 'But my people are dying, and I don't have the time for this crap.'

The news of Akimiri's death rippled through the massed Annihilators, and from that moment on, the battle turned into a mere exercise of extermination.

The human warriors cut and killed without pause, delivering death without showing mercy or quarter.

And as the sun lay heavy above the horizon, waiting before it gave way to the blue light of the moon, the final alien was eradicated.

The scourge of the Annihilators was over, and the earth ran red with the blood of the fallen. Fully eighty thousand bodies lay on the field of battle. Eighty thousand vanquished souls.

Sixty thousand Annihilator warriors. Ten thousand flying Yari.

And ten thousand men who had paid the ultimate price for humanity's freedom.

Tad and Kob walked over to Nathaniel. Both were covered in blood, their own and the enemy's.

'Well your people weren't much help,' said Tad, speaking to the Orc.

'They are not my people,' grunted Kob.

'Whatever,' continued Tad. 'You know what I mean. The only thing that the Fair-Folk didn't do was actually run away.'

Kob didn't answer. He merely stood staring at the mass of the Fair-Folk army that had now marched much closer.

'Oh, here they come,' said Tad. 'Now that the battle is over they finally begin to move. Idiots,' he snapped.

Still Kob didn't react, he simply

continued staring, his eyes narrowed to slits. He raised his hand to shield his sight from the setting sun.

Then suddenly he shouted out loud. ‘Look to the archers,’ he cried. ‘Take cover.’ He grabbed Nathaniel by the arm. ‘Betrayal!’

And the rays of the setting sun were blotted out as a storm of arrows was unleashed by the goblin archers, arcing through the air towards the human survivors. The goblins fired again and again, filling the sky with a swarm of steel-tipped death. By the time the first volley of arrows struck home, there were already another three hundred thousand in the air.

Human warriors threw up their shields in an effort to protect themselves, and the sound of steel ripping into flesh and shattering shields was overwhelming.

‘Form up,’ shouted Tad. ‘On me, shields up. Form a tortoise.’

Humans gathered together in packs of twenty and thirty, overlocking their shields above their heads to form an arrow-proof

roof. But many were being struck down by an arrow storm the likes of which none had ever seen before.

Then the ground shook as half a million Orcs began their charge, bearing down on the exhausted humans like a wave of rushing death.

And, at the rear of the Fair-Folk army, Ammon and Seth congratulated each other. The plan that they had formulated after they had seen The Forever Man's weapon display had worked perfectly. It had been a gamble; they had to assume that the humans would use up all of their ammunition. They assumed that the humans would win, and finally, they had assumed that the win would exhaust the human warriors to such an extent that it would be relatively easy to overwhelm them.

In one fell swoop they had gotten rid of all of their enemies. It was now only a matter of time before the five hundred thousand Orcs dispatched the broken human warriors and ended their resistance forever.

Nathaniel saw the Orc horde charging in, and something in him snapped. He could actually feel it happen, like a boat breaking free of its moorings in a storm, or a wild horse slipping its halter. His mind left the confinements of his consciousness and expanded across the land, drawing in prodigious quantities of power from the pulse light.

Heat boiled off him in waves, so hot that the snow around him melted and evaporated in billowing clouds of steam. The air shimmered and flashing colors coalesced about him as lightning bolts crackled through him, short-circuiting into the earth with explosions as loud as thunder.

Then the very earth itself started to crack and buckle and heave as it shook violently.

'No!' shouted The Forever Man. And his voice thundered across the battlefield like a clarion call.

'I will not allow this to happen.'

He raised his arms and spread them

wide, grimacing in pain as untold quantities of pulse-power rushed into him. His nose started to bleed as the surfeit of power threatened to literally tear him apart.

And then he spoke.

'Shield,' he commanded.

A translucent dome appeared above the humans and the goblin arrows simply bounced off it and skittered down the side, unable to penetrate.

'Fire,' he commanded.

A wall of flame rose up between the charging Orcs and the human survivors. Blood started to pour from Nathaniel's ears as his brain began to rupture under the strain.

'Nathaniel,' yelled Tad. 'Stop it. You're killing yourself.'

'Wind,' commanded The Forever Man.

And a group of small tornados sprang up and started to push the wall of fire towards the Orcs, forcing them back.

Blood began to flow from the

Marine's eyes, and he fell to his knees and then fell forward, as waves of unbearable pain drove him to the floor.

Tad tried to grab him and support him, but as he touched the Marine his hands were seared from the heat and he had to pull back, his palms red and blistered.

The Forever Man's clothes started to smolder and burn, but still he persisted, pushing the Fair-Folk army back.

'Stop it,' shouted Tad. 'Please, Nathaniel. Stop, before you die.'

Kob grabbed the Little Big Man by the shoulder. 'Come, my friend,' he said. 'We must use this time to retreat back behind the wall. If we do not, then his sacrifice will have been for nothing.'

'I'm not leaving him,' said Tad as he tried once again to grab Nathaniel, but he had to pull back as the heat raised more blisters in his hands and arms.

'Go,' repeated Kob. 'Gather the men. They need a leader. But do not worry, I will keep The Forever Man safe, you have my word.'

Tad nodded and set to gathering the men together and getting them to the wall while the pillars of flame still held the Fair-Folk army back.

The Free State warriors flooded back to the wall, crowding through the gates, and running to the top of the wall to defend against any attack that transpired after the flames had died down.

Tad glanced up to see Grim-son flaring his wings to land on the battlement. He folded his wings and walked over to The Little Big Man. 'What is happ-ening?' he asked in his staccato accent. 'We saw flames, so we have come.'

'Good,' replied Tad. 'We have been betrayed by the Fair-Folk. As soon as the Annihilators had been vanquished the Fair-Folk turned on us. Nathaniel magiked up a wall of flame so that we could escape, but he's still out there. He's with Kob.'

'We have brought more fire-bombs with us, so we can provide air supp-ort,' said Grim-son as he unfurled his wings and leapt into the sky. 'If the Fair-Folk push their attack they will rue the day. We may be diminish-ed, but we will still burn them from the field of battle.'

Without warning, the wall of flames and the tornadoes winked out of existence. Tad saw Kob pick The Forever Man up and run for the gates, holding the Marine in his arms like a broken doll.

As the Orc got closer, Tad could see that Nathaniel was still giving off massive quantities of heat. Kob's skin was burned and blistered and his leather armor was smoking. Tad realized that the pain must be immense, and he marveled at Kob's ability to keep functioning despite the terrible injuries he was causing himself.

As soon as he ran through the gates they were closed behind him and he laid Nathaniel's smoking body on the ground. Roo ran over and threw a bucket of water over Kob and Nathaniel and the water sputtered and steamed as it hit them.

On the wall, Tad had rallied the archers and they were ready, bows strung, waiting for the Orc charge. Above, the Vandals circled, ready to drop their flasks of fire.

But no charge came.

Commander Ammon knew that he had lost the initiative and he was unsure of how injured The Forever Man was. He would not risk his troops to be subjected to a storm of fire that could, quite possibly, wipe them out completely. So, he ordered his army to stand down and pull back. There would be time later. The humans had taken a dreadful battering and this war was far from over.

The human army had been decimated. Of the thirty-eight thousand men who had fought in that final battle only ten thousand remained. And the cavalry had been wiped out completely, destroyed by the goblin arrow storms. There was not one family that had not lost someone, father, grandfather, son, mother, or daughter.

The Vandals had lost fully half of their able-bodied flyers and of that half, many were badly injured.

With a heavy heart, Tad came to realize that their numbers were too few to man Hadrian's Wall any longer. So, he gave his order to retreat to the Antonine Wall. In the heavy snow and sleet, the last surviving humans trudged northwards, leaving their farms and their houses behind, taking only what they could carry, their carts full of the wounded and dying survivors.

And in the one cart, swaddled in furs, was the corpse of Nathaniel Hogan. Once a king, once a Marine, and once known as The Forever Man.

Tad refused to acknowledge Nathaniel's death.

'Gogo will cure him,' he said. 'He'll come back to us,' his face wet with tears and his eyes bloodshot from constant weeping. And none dared gainsay his belief for, like him, the death of their leader was simply too much to comprehend. He had been humanity's rock. Their shelter from the storm and their only light in a world gone dark.

But when the column of refugees finally reached the wall and Gogo had seen Nathaniel's body she had merely shaken her head and turned away.

There was nothing that she could do. He was gone.

There was no wake for The Forever Man like there had been for Papa Dante.

No party, no speeches. The clocks were stopped, and the bells muffled. Candles and torches were extinguished, and no food but bread and water was served in any household.

The body was wrapped in pure white linen and laid at the foot of the Tomnavarie standing stone. For two days people filed past and the sound of weeping could be heard from over a mile away.

On the third day, there was a storm the likes of which had never been seen before in living memory.

Thunder tore apart the sky and jagged bolts of lightning stitched it back together. Snow and sleet were driven across the land by shrieking winds and the pulse lights flared and sparkled in the heavens like God's fireworks.

The next day, when the mourners struggled through the snow drifts to the standing stone, they arrived to find that the body was gone.

But the linen shroud was still there.

Tad allowed himself a small smile.

There were two moons in the sky.

And the sun seemed closer. Larger.

The air smelled of snow, and when he looked through the open window he could see why. A large mountain loomed over the house, its peak capped in white. Outside a cherry tree shed its blossoms as the wind ruffled its branches. The floor below the tree, a carpet of pink. Beyond it, a wide stream, clear and sparkling with little shards of ice.

He looked around the room that he was in. Walls consisted of rice paper between black-lacquered wood frames. A pitched ceiling and floors of highly polished cedar wood.

The bed that he had just risen from was a futon that lay directly on the floor in the center of the room. On the side, next to the door, stood a washstand. On it, a ceramic bowl of blue and white, a pitcher of water, and a vase containing a single white orchid.

He was dressed in a loose black tunic and matching black trousers woven from the finest silk.

His axe was nowhere to be seen.

There was a soft knock on the door and it was opened before he could speak. A man walked in. He was dressed in a similar fashion, his long gray hair tied up in a bun on the top of his head. Long gray mustache and beard, neatly combed.

He was quite obviously old, but his face was unlined and his eyes seemed to shift in color, one moment obsidian and the next a winter's blue.

He bowed. 'Good,' he said. 'You are awake.'

Nathaniel nodded but said nothing.

'You must be hungry, and also have many questions.'

Again, the Marine nodded, but stayed quiet.

The old man clapped his hands twice and two more men entered the room. They were dressed in short red robes and their demeanor was that of a servant. Or perhaps a novice, their manner less about subservience and more about respect. They were carrying a large tray. On the tray were two covered bowls, a tea pot, some cups, and chopsticks.

They lay the tray on the floor and left, after bowing low.

The old man sat down, cross-legged, in front of the tray and gestured to Nathaniel to do the same.

The Marine did so. Then he spoke.

'I died.'

The old man smiled. 'But you are hungry?' he asked.

'Yes.'

'Do the dead feel hunger?' Continued the old man.

Nathaniel shrugged. 'Perhaps. How

would I know? I've never been dead before.'

'Strictly speaking, that is not true,' said the old man. 'Technically, you have died many times; you have simply been resurrected afterwards.'

'Whatever,' said the Marine. 'This time was different. I could feel myself dying. I felt the lights go out. I am dead.'

The old man nodded. 'Yes, you are correct. This time it was different. This time you are deader than before.'

'So, what next?'

'Next,' said the old man. 'We eat,' and he waved at the bowls before he poured some green tea into the two cups.

Nathaniel took the lid off one of the bowls. It contained plain boiled white rice. He tried the next one. It was the same. So, he picked up his chopsticks and proceeded to eat, sipping the tea as he did so.

The old man ate as well, holding the bowl close to his mouth and using the chopsticks to shovel the rice in.

Afterwards, Nathaniel felt much better as the carbohydrates picked up his energy levels.

'Okay,' he said. 'So, I am deader than before. Where am I?'

The old man smiled. 'A good question. Unfortunately, one that is very difficult to answer, however, I shall make an attempt. But first, where do you think that you are?'

'Judging by the two moons, another planet. Not Earth. But the architecture and the scenery seem Japanese. Or at least sort of Japanese. Perhaps some sort of holy retreat. Buddhist monks? And that is about as good a guess as I can come up with. So, I ask again, where am I?'

'You are not on another planet, as such,' said the old man. 'Nor are you in Japan. You are simply existing on a separate plane to the one that you were in, on Earth. The surroundings are a construct of your own mind. Your mind has constructed two moons in order to tell you that you are in a different place. You have created a tranquil environment in which to recover and to learn. Hence the cherry blossoms, the religious atmosphere, the plain food. My appearance.'

'Your appearance?' questioned Nathaniel. 'Who are you?'

'We have met many times before,' said the old man. 'But those times your mind saw me as a creature of myth and legend. It constructed an effigy that was in conjunction with the information that you were receiving.'

Nathaniel nodded. 'So,' he said. 'You are The Unicorn.'

'Very quick,' agreed the old man. 'I was. I am.'

'But now you are some sort of old Kung Fu master who shall guide me and teach me.' said Nathaniel.

The old man nodded.

'So, what do I call you?' asked Nathaniel. 'Master? Teacher? Sensei?'

'I have many names, but you can call me Fulcrum.'

‘Why Fulcrum?’

‘Have you heard of a man called Archimedes?’

Nathaniel nodded. ‘Greek dude. Mathematician, lived real long ago.’

‘That’s the one,’ confirmed the old man. ‘He once said; Give me a lever long enough and a fulcrum on which to place it and I shall move the world. Well, I am that fulcrum.’

‘And the lever?’ asked the Marine.

Fulcrum smiled. ‘You are the lever. And together we shall move the world.’

‘I see. So, have you done this sort of thing before?’

Fulcrum nodded. ‘Many, many times throughout human history.’

‘So, how come I’ve never heard of you?’

‘Oh, you have,’ said Fulcrum. ‘But under many different names. I was once known as Anaxarchus. Under that name I tutored Alexander the Great.’

'I thought that was Aristotle,' countered Nathaniel.

'You know your history,' answered Fulcrum. 'It is true, Aristotle tutored Alexander. As did Clearchus of Soli and Leonidas of Epirus. But Anaxarchus was Alexander's personal friend. I was his companion throughout all of his campaigns. Together we moved the world. In the fifteen hundreds, I was known as Jean de Chavigny, a close personal friend and advisor to Nostradamus. At another time I was Joshua Speed, confidant and friend to Abraham Lincoln. For a few years, I trod the boards as Henry Condell, William Shakespeare's friend and muse. I can give many more examples,' said Fulcrum. 'But I am sure that you get the point. I have seen the birth of many great things and played a central role therein.'

'And now, it's my turn,' said Nathaniel.

'Now, it is your turn,' acknowledged Fulcrum.

'So, what do we do next?'

‘Next,’ answered Fulcrum. ‘I teach, and you learn. It shall not be an easy road, but it is a necessary one. Are you willing to learn?’

Nathaniel nodded.

‘Good. Now, development of the mind can be accomplished only when the body has been disciplined. We shall start with that. Follow me.’

Fulcrum stood up and left the room.

The Forever Man followed.

Tad was now the leader of the Free State, or what was left of it. After the death of their king the people had unanimously called on The Little Big Man to lead them. In fact, they had called on him to become king.

He had accepted the role of leader but had refused to be crowned. Instead, he had hung the crown in his meeting room next to Nathaniel's axe. They dominated the room with their presence, a solid reminder of their leader that was.

Over the last month, Tad had reinforced the Antonine Wall with extra towers and barracks for the Vandal flyers. And the shorter length of the wall combined with its strategic position had kept the remaining humans alive as they were able to defend against the ensuing

Orc attacks.

When Nathaniel had insisted that they build the Antonine Wall, taking men from the defense of Hadrian's Wall, people had obeyed, but there had been much muttering. They wondered why their leader had requested such folly. And why he had done so at such a crucial time. Now, however, his far-sighted order followed by his heroic death and subsequent disappearance had raised The Forever Man to the level of a demigod in the eyes of his people.

When Tad had accepted the position of leader of the new Free State, thereby leaving his position of head of the army, he had done so under one condition. And that was him being able to appoint his successor as head of defense. People had agreed, and the Little Big Man had not hesitated in appointing Orc Master Sergeant Kob, thereby elevating him to the rank of general.

There was no opposition to Kob's appointment, his heroic attempt to save Nathaniel, carrying his burning body back in his arms and suffering third-degree burns himself, was still fresh in people's minds. The Orc was a hero, and the people told him that he had been accepted as an honorary human. Kob argued, in his usual blank-faced way, that he would rather accept the humans as honorary Orcs.

Tad had then put Roo and Sam, the leader of the walking people, in charge of food and housing. Roo had recommended setting up a collective farming and living system that he called Gatherings.

Each Gathering would consist of around one hundred extended family units, including siblings, grandparents, uncles, and aunts. This equated to Gatherings of between six hundred and one thousand people. Roo considered this to be the optimal size for a Gathering to work as a semi-autonomous unit.

Each Gathering would allocate farm work, hunting, cloth production, building and so forth to various different families who would then specialize in those occupations. Meals would be taken in communal halls. Childcare, lessons, and discipline would be carried out by groups allocated to the task which would leave the parents free to concentrate on building their community or providing food.

Twenty percent of all combat-ready members were allocated to wall defense on a full-time basis and these members could be rotated if need be.

All people in the Gatherings were allocated a minimum of three hours free time a day during which they were encouraged to concentrate on military skills ranging from actual combat through to tracking, study of tactics, or the practicalities of fletching or blade making.

When the call was given, then each Gathering would send all of their able-bodied combatants to obey the call. No differentiation was made between men and women. The gathering had its own military structure from sergeants up to lieutenants. When pulled together into an army, an appointed captain was put in charge of three gatherings which formed a Division. Three of these Divisions were termed a Battalion, and a colonel would be put in charge of each Battalion.

The Vandals kept up a constant air patrol along the wall, ensuring that any Orc attacks were reported well in advance. Without them, Tad was convinced that the humans would not have survived, and they would be forever indebted to the flying creatures.

It was taking time and effort to institute the new way of living, but on the whole, it seemed to bode well. People were happy, and the system worked.

Tad was not convinced that it was the way to live forever, but for the foreseeable future, the discipline and regulation was necessary for humanity's ongoing survival.

The Little Big Man massaged his temples and drew in a deep breath. He was exhausted but so was everybody else. The constant work and alertness pushed everyone to their limits, and there was never any chance of respite.

Vigilance was their watchword and hard work was their way of life. Weapons of war were humanity's new art form and the wielding of said weapons was their new dance.

The front door to Tad's small house banged open and he heard the rap of running feet. Immediately his face bloomed into a wide smile, his tension headache forgotten as Clare and Stephanie barreled into the room.

'Hi, Dad,' they both greeted in unison. Clare handed him an arrow, a full-length cloth-yard shaft with goose feather fletching.

'I made this for you,' she said.

Tad held it up to his eyes and checked it closely. It was a fantastic job. Well made with Clare's usual care and attention to detail.

'I did this,' chimed Stephanie, as she plunked a loaf of what was most probably bread on the table. It was lopsided and had not risen properly and the one end was slightly scorched. Unlike her sister, Stephanie treated her practical lessons as a necessary evil that should be finished as quickly as possible regardless of the quality of the end product. However, she excelled in book work, her reading and writing already at a level that rivaled the teachers themselves.

'Have you eaten yet?' asked Clare.

Tad shook his head.

'I'll make us lunch,' she continued. 'I can use Stephanie's bread to make cheese sandwiches.'

'It won't taste any good,' said Stephanie. 'My bread never does.'

'It'll be fine,' argued Clare. 'We'll just cut off the burned bits.'

'And the hard bits and the unbaked bits,' added Stephanie. 'There won't be much left.'

'There'll be enough,' said Clare as the two of them headed for the kitchen area.

Tad watched them go, his face still all agrin, their mere presence a balm for his dog-tired mind and body.

Nathaniel's body had literally turned blue. He had been standing under the waterfall since sunrise. Eight hours ago. The sheer volume of water almost overwhelmed him, making it difficult to breathe, and almost impossible to stand, as the tons of water pummeled his back and shoulders. But the cold was the worst part of the ordeal. The water was below freezing, and small shards of ice were mixed with it. Only the rapid water movement was keeping it from freezing solid.

When Fulcrum had first led The Forever Man out to the waterfall and bid him stand under it, he had lasted less than a minute. It was simply totally debilitating. When a human body is immersed in freezing cold water it immediately starts to shut down. Some victims die within minutes due to loss of breath or heart failure. Stronger, fitter people will last longer. But no one will last as long as one hour before severe hypothermia sets in and organ shutdown begins.

Initially, Nathaniel had attempted to draw heat in from his surrounds, using the pulse power to heat the water up. But Fulcrum had snapped at him, telling him that he was not there to perform parlor tricks.

'Look into yourself, Nathaniel,' he had urged. 'This is not about magiks, it is about you.'

The Marine was baffled. How was he meant to stand under the water without either dying or simply stepping out?

Fulcrum had simply told him that he had to stand under the waterfall all day and he would not be allowed to proceed any further in his training until he did so.

So, every morning, The Forever Man would rise before the sun, take a simple breakfast of plain rice and green tea, and proceed to the waterfall.

And then he would force himself to stand under the freezing water until severe hypothermia set in and he died.

He would wake later, back in his bed, wrapped in furs, his head throbbing like a jackhammer. Next to him a meal of broth and rice and tea. He would eat. Fulcrum would enter the room and talk until nightfall.

He would sleep.

The next morning, he would go back to the waterfall and die again.

And even though he tried his hardest, willing himself to live through the experience, he never lasted more than one hour.

One evening, Fulcrum entered the room and sat down cross-legged opposite Nathaniel as he had done for the past sixty-two nights.

'Albert Einstein once said to me, to do the same thing, over and over again and to expect different results, is the very definition of insanity.'

'It's impossible to do,' mumbled Nathaniel. 'A human body simply can't stop itself freezing. If you allowed me to use the power to heat myself up, then it would be easy.'

Fulcrum shook his head. 'In the year 2000, before the pulse, a magician called David Blaine encased himself in ice for over sixty-five hours and lived. The Shingon Buddhists stand for many hours under ice-cold waterfalls in temperatures of minus three degrees. So, it is possible.'

'Well then, tell me how to do it,' said Nathaniel.

Fulcrum shook his head. 'No. Look inside yourself. You can do it, and you will do it. We shall try again tomorrow. I shall pick you up at sunrise.'

And that sunrise had been eight hours ago.

That morning, Nathanial had entered the waterfall, and instead of fighting the cold, he accepted it. He let it flow through him, concentrating his energy into a kernel in the center of his being, apart from all else. An entity in itself. A reactor that he could call into service at a later stage.

And then he let his mind go free, leaving his body almost entirely, simply keeping a simple spark of life ready to fire back up when he returned.

Fulcrum called him after ten hours by standing on the bank and beckoning. Nathaniel brought his consciousness back into his body and then forced the kernel of energy to expand through him. The cold came smashing back, freezing his brain, his blood, and his inner organs. But he commanded his legs to move, and with shaking footsteps, he staggered from the water.

Fulcrum threw a fur around the Marine's shoulders.

'Well done, Nathaniel,' he said. 'You have opened the gateway to your education.'

The Forever Man didn't say anything. All conversation precluded by the chattering of his teeth.

The next morning when he woke,

instead of dry rice, he found a bowl of fish stew, freshly squeezed fruit juice, dark bread, and preserves. A veritable feast.

When he had finished, the door was opened, and instead of Fulcrum, another ancient man walked in. He was attired in a similar fashion to Fulcrum and his hair and beard were the same, although longer and thinner.

He bowed to Nathaniel and then gestured for him to follow.

The Marine rose and went with the ancient man. The man walked with the aid of a staff, a long, gnarled length of unpolished oak about seven feet long, almost two feet taller than the man himself. They followed the stream for about a mile and then stopped.

The old man pointed at a wooden post. It was standing upright, around Nathaniel's shoulder height. About six inches in diameter, the top slightly convex. A shallow dome shape. When Nathaniel took a closer look, he could see that the top of the pole had been greased with some sort of animal fat.

The old man tapped the top of the pole with his staff and spoke for the first time.

'Stand on here. One foot only.'

Nathaniel laughed. 'Yeah, sure. That's impossible, it's greased up and it's a dome.'

The Marine didn't even see the ancient man move; he simply felt the crack of the oak staff against his head and felt the blood run down into his eyes.

'Stand here,' repeated the man as he tapped the pole again.

'How the hell did you move so fast?' asked Nathaniel in amazement.

'Not so fast,' replied the ancient man. 'You just slow. Now, stand on pole.'

Nathaniel shook his head, walked up to the pole, and attempted to climb onto it. But the shape and the grease defeated him.

The old man poked him in the back with his staff. 'Get up. Stand. One foot.'

‘Hey, old dude,’ snapped Nathaniel. ‘Quit poking me with that stick or I’ll smack you around a bit.’

‘Ha!’ exclaimed the ancient one. ‘In your dreams, snail boy.’ The staff whistled through the air and connected with the Marine’s shoulder.

Once again Nathaniel didn’t see it coming, even though he was waiting for it.

‘Okay. I’ll try again.’ Nathaniel took a run and jumped up onto the top of the pole, slipped and came crashing down. This time the staff connected with the back of his head.

‘Quit it.’

‘Stand on pole.’

‘Why?’ asked Nathaniel.

‘Do you wish to learn?’ countered the old man.

‘Yes.’

‘Well then,’ continued the old man. ‘Stand on pole.’

This time the staff cracked against

Nathaniel's shins.

By the time the two suns started to sink below the mountain, Nathaniel was as battered and bruised and bleeding as if he had fought a battle.

He had still not managed to gain the top of the pole.

He limped home with the ancient man and his oaken staff. When they got to Nathanial's residence the old man bowed.

'Endurance is one of the most difficult disciplines, but it is to the one that endures that the final victory comes.' He jabbed Nathaniel one more time with the point of his staff. 'You may call me, Caritas. I shall see you tomorrow morning; we will continue your training.'

Milly held up her hand. ‘Enough,’ she said. ‘I shall pass judgment. Will the accused stand?’

A young man stood up. His wrists were manacled together, as were his ankles. His one eye was swollen shut and his hair stood up in jagged spikes, fashioned there by dried blood.

‘This court of law finds you guilty of both sedition and the worship and advocation of the false God,’ proclaimed Milly. ‘As such you shall be taken from this court and hung by the neck until dead. Do you have any last words?’

‘There is no crueler tyranny than that which is perpetuated under the shield of law and the name of justice,’ answered the man.

‘Take him away,’ commanded Milly.

Two Orcs grabbed the accused by his arms and dragged him towards the door.

‘There is a higher court than this,’ the man shouted as they manhandled him down the aisle. ‘It is the court of conscience and soon you shall be tried by it.’

Milly stood up and waited for one of her human servants to place her fur cloak around her shoulders. She knew that some were of the opinion that she had too many servants, but she figured that she was entitled to them. In fact, it was a necessity as opposed to a luxury. Being the paramount human in the Fair-Folk realm, she literally worked an eighteen hour plus day.

Since the Great Victory, when Commander Ammon and his army had vanquished the Annihilators and simultaneously forced the renegade humans back to the far north of the country, Milly had thrown herself into her work.

It had been rumored that Nathaniel had been slain in the battle, but as there were no actual eye witnesses to his death, Milly took the news with a pinch of salt. She fervently hoped that it was true, but suspected that he was simply lying low, licking his wounds after his humiliating defeat by the brave Commander Ammon and the Orc army.

Be that as it may, Milly had taken the opportunity to mold a new regime. A new structure for the humans that now fell under the Fair-Folk leadership. She no longer had to worry about Nathaniel and his people attacking them and ruining all that they had achieved.

There would be no more warmongering and pedaling of hatred. Laws would be obeyed, and humanity would prosper under the benign dictatorship of the Fair-Folk with her at the helm of all human affairs.

The first thing that Milly had done was to eradicate all of the existing human rank structures. There were no longer humans, worthy humans, and superior humans. Now there were simply humans. And in charge of them all—Milly, the paramount human. Humans were no longer given any form of control of anything above menial labor and servitude. It was necessary, she had explained to Ammon. They simply could not be trusted with any power whatsoever as they would merely abuse it. It was harsh, but it was the only way to ensure their own safety in the long run.

She also banned private ownership of anything bar clothing. They were housed in communal dwellings, ate in communal halls, and all of their labor was supervised by goblin overseers.

Milly had also forbidden meetings, public speaking, and religious worship. All of these fell under the umbrella of sedition and were punishable by death.

As a result of these draconian measures human crime had been almost totally eradicated, not counting the crime of sedition.

Humanity was finally at peace, and

Milly knew that it was mainly due to her.

Unbeknown to Milly, Commander Ammon stood in the shadows at the back of the hall of justice and watched her leave. Once again, he was impressed at the cold way that she dispensed justice to her own kind. Her judgments were swift and taken without vacillation or indecision.

Truth be known, Ammon had a great deal of respect for human Milly. If only she wasn't so horrifically unattractive, he thought to himself. That pinkish skin and all of that hair. Horrendous. He shuddered.

But apart from his unrequited feelings towards the paramount human he was genuinely and completely happy. The Fair-Folk had consolidated their position and the humans were no longer a threat. As far as Seth and his mages could tell, The Forever Man was no more, and the human numbers had fallen to such a level that they could barely defend their new wall, let alone conduct any aggressive forays.

So, the Fair-Folk, and particularly their commander, now lived a life of unparalleled luxury unheard of in their living memories.

Perhaps in the future they would launch an attack against the humans and then finally subjugate them entirely—but for now, they would simply wallow in their well-deserved comfort.

Ammon pulled himself from his reverie and went outside, followed by his Orc bodyguards. He picked up his pace a little as he left. After all, he had a front seat and he didn't want to miss the hanging.

Nathaniel sprinted along the bank of the stream. He was barefoot and wearing only a pair of silk shorts. He reached the greased pole, leapt onto it, and stopped. Dead still. He stood on one foot, the other raised to his chest, then he swapped, leaping high into the air as he did so.

After a minute of balancing he sprang to the ground and continued his run, first crossing the stream on a tightrope, running along it with sure foot and perfect balance.

On the other side of the stream was a track that all referred to as 'the path of pain'. It was covered in shards of razor-sharp flint, capable of slashing deeply into a man's foot. The Marine ran over it without any sign of hurt or discomfort.

Next, he ran to the mountain,

sprinting upwards, leaping from rock to rock until the incline got so steep that he had to run on all fours, and then eventually, he started to climb the perpendicular rock face, finding handholds that seemed, to the naked eye, to be nothing more than a dimple in the rock.

Finally, he reached the top and stood on the peak, snow and sleet blew at him in savage gusts and his torso glistened with a coating of frozen sweat.

After catching his breath, he started down the mountain, soaring from rock to rock, feet hardly touching the earth as he tore down the steep incline.

An hour later he stood outside his dwelling, steaming like a race horse as he stood in the cold to recover. But before he could catch his breath, five acolytes, young men ranging between twenty and twenty-five, stepped out from the bushes. Each was armed with a six-foot staff. As one, they attacked the Marine, stout staffs whistling through the air fast enough to break bone and crush flesh on contact.

But the Marine was as smoke, impossible to strike as he whirled and jumped. Then, with explosive speed, he lashed out. In less than a second, all five of the acolytes were on the ground, unconscious.

Fulcrum came out of the building and nodded. 'Well done,' he said. 'As I said in the beginning, development of the mind can be accomplished only when the body has been disciplined. The physical part of your training is now complete. It is time to learn about real power.'

Nathaniel's teacher walked towards the stream and then turned to follow a track that would take them through the cherry tree orchards and to a small set of standing stones. There were nine stones, about seven feet high and set in a circle. Some had faded glyphs carved into them, swirls and geometric patterns.

In the center of the circle a large flat stone lay on its side, a perfect height for a bench. Fulcrum sat down and beckoned to Nathaniel to do the same.

'Up to now,' said Fulcrum. 'I have advised against you using magik to complete your given tasks.'

'Well, if by advised you actually mean banned, then I agree,' said Nathaniel.

Fulcrum allowed himself the glimmer of a smile. 'I did this for a reason. You had to hone your physical skills first in order to allow your spiritual side to follow. Now, for the first time, I would like you to conjure up a small ball of fire. Nothing too ostentatious, something the size of your fist will do.'

The Marine concentrated, pulled in power and created a flaming ball. It hovered in front of the two of them, giving off a smoky orange glare.

'Good,' said Fulcrum. 'Now, how did you do that?'

'Easy,' replied Nathaniel. 'I simply pulled in power from the pulse light and turned it into energy in the form of fire.'

Fulcrum nodded. 'Could you create a ball of ice?'

'Probably,' said Nathaniel. 'Not so good with ice. Never saw a need. There's always snow around anyhow. I can do light. I've done wind before but can't actually remember how. It was a heat of battle sort of thing.'

'Magik very basic,' said Fulcrum. 'Firstly, one must realize that it is not a given thing. Some can do it and others cannot, much like some are gifted with phenomenal eyesight and some are shortsighted. The ability is a biological imperative. You have been gifted with an almost limitless ability within you. To put it bluntly, you are a freak of nature. But you are, at present, an amateur. An unguided missile. Basically, a dumb bomb.'

'Oh, thanks,' quipped Nathaniel. 'You forgot to tell me that my mother dresses me funny and that I have the intellect of a stoat.'

'I do not mean to insult,' mollified Fulcrum. 'I am merely pointing out the truth. You wield a power that you have no real knowledge about. For example, where does the power come from and what makes it possible to use?'

Nathaniel thought for a few moments before he answered. 'I get the power from the pulse light. I simply concentrate on it, pull it in and then release it in the form that I want.'

'Basically correct,' acknowledged Fulcrum. 'Although very basically. Your explanation is much like saying that one gets wet in the rain because water makes you wet. True, but without any understanding of water at all.

Your power does stem from the pulse light. But what you do not know is that different power is gained through different colors. Red, orange, yellow, green, blue, indigo, and violet,' Fulcrum spread his arms and a rainbow appeared in front of them, its colors bright and vibrant.

'But there are more colors than those obvious ones. Think of color like sound, there are sounds that the human ear cannot hear, but we do experience them. These sounds are either too deep or too high for our usual range of hearing. However, contradictorily, they are the most powerful of sounds. Deep notes, around nine Hz, will produce nausea, anxiety, shortness of breath. High notes can shatter glass, damage human cell structure, and cause physiological damage. It is the same with color; the ones that we cannot see are the most powerful ones. And I am not talking about different wavelengths like infra-red and ultra violet.' He clicked his fingers and the colors in the rainbow separated into individual arcs.

'I am talking about the two colors on either side of the visible spectrum. *Crimrow*, red, orange, yellow, green, blue, indigo, violet, *zylac*.

These are the most important lights. Crimrow is referred to as the chaste-light. Zylac is the sub-light or black-light. Crimrow brings life and Zylac encourages death. Green is earth-light, growth and peace. Hot colors, red, orange, yellow, are heat-light. Fire, warmth, power through heat, flying, movement, fireballs.'

Nathaniel held up his hand. 'Whoa.

Information dump. Slow down. Okay—so, from what you are saying, it's pretty obvious. Hot colors are hot and cold colors are cold. I get that. Crimrow and zylac are the important lights but I can't see them. So, how am I going to use them?'

Fulcrum smiled. 'You are already using these lights at an unconscious level. To you it is like breathing. Or keeping your heart beating. You don't have to think about it. It is an autonomous thing. It simply happens. However, I will teach you how to control it.'

'How am I already using them?' asked Nathaniel. 'What do I do with them?'

'You use them at a sub-atomic level, constantly vacillating between the one and the other. That is why you are immortal. When you die you embrace death via the sub-light. This keeps your body in a state of suspended animation while the chaste-light repairs your body, bringing you back to life. Your enhanced speed and strength are brought about through your unconscious use of both the earth-lights and the heat-light.'

'I was told by a Nobel Prize winning professor once that it was Gamma rays that enhanced my speed,' argued Nathaniel.

Fulcrum nodded. 'Same thing, different terminology.'

'Whatever,' conceded the Marine. 'When do we start?'

'To coin a cliché,' said Fulcrum. 'No time like the present. But before we do, there is one more thing that you have to know. And it is very important. The pulse light, or life light is your source of power, but without the standing stones it is very weak.'

'Come again,' said Nathaniel.

'The standing stones,' repeated Fulcrum. 'Stonehenge, the Seven Sisters, Castlerigg, Ringmoor.'

'I get it,' interrupted Nathaniel. 'I know that the stones are some sort of portal. The rubber heads came through one in Cornwall. I suspect the Annihilators did the same. But how do they affect the power?'

'Have you heard about ley lines?' asked Fulcrum.

'Vaguely,' admitted Nathanial. 'Some sort of pathway that connects ancient monuments or such.'

'Not quite,' corrected Fulcrum. 'A ley line is a magnetic path of power that connects all ancient places of power. Stone circles, cathedrals, places of worship. People have come up with many theories as to what these ley lines represent, and some have even gotten quite close. But I can tell you that they are conduits. Imagine, if you will, that the stones circles are points of power, like batteries. Each, on its own, is not that powerful, however, all of them connected together are capable of producing an almost unbelievable amount of power.

The ley lines are the cables that would connect these batteries. So, when you draw power from the life light you don't only draw power from your direct vicinity, you actually draw power from every point on the compass that is connected via the ley lines. Like a fisherman casting a net as opposed to a single line.'

'So, if there were no standing stones?' asked Nathaniel. 'Would magik be possible?'

'Oh yes,' answered Fulcrum. 'However, let me put it in perspective. There are around ten thousand standing stone sites in the United Kingdom. Ten thousand separate sources of power that is multiplied via the ley lines. Without those, the power that you could concentrate would be tiny. Enough to provide light, fire. Your speed

and ability to heal would still work as it uses little power but it uses it constantly. Essentially, without ley lines you would be an almost immortal, exceptional warrior capable of some very impressive parlor tricks.'

'Okay,' said Nathaniel. 'Let's do it.'

'First, you need to learn how to see, or at least become aware of the invisible lights, crimrow, and zylac.'

‘How long will it take?’ enquired the Marine.

Fulcrum raised an eyebrow. ‘It will take as long as it takes. Suffice to say, you shall have to learn how to listen for the color of the sky. Look for the sound of the hummingbird's wings. Search the air for the perfume of ice on a hot day. When you have found these things, you will find an awareness of the hidden colors.’

‘That is impossible.’

Fulcrum shrugged. ‘For many it is. But as the Persian poet, Saadi once said; you must have patience, for all things are difficult before they become easy.’

‘Yeah well, as Confucius once said—just because man has one, does not mean he has to act like one,’ answered Nathaniel sarcastically.

Fulcrum smiled. ‘Let us begin.’

Once again Kob had disobeyed a direct order from Tad. The Little Big Man had expressly forbidden anyone venturing into enemy territory for any reason whatsoever.

Over the last few years an uneasy truce had built up between the humans and the Fair-Folk. Humans stuck to their side of the wall and the Fair-Folk, on the whole, left them alone. However, a small but constant stream of escaped humans arrived at the wall to seek asylum. Humans who had broken free from the Fair-Folk pens, killing their Orc guards, and fleeing for the Free State.

If they managed to make the wall, then Tad always took them in. On the other hand, he forbade any humans actually going into rubber head territory to physically help the refugees. Tad maintained that there were barely enough human warriors to man the wall, let alone take on a Fair-Folk invasion if Ammon decided to punish them for helping human renegades.

Kob had argued, repeating stories of horrific Fair-Folk abuse of humans. Keeping them in cages little bigger than dog kennels. Feeding them on gruel and grass cuttings. Literally working them to death.

Tad had merely shaken his head. 'I must protect what we have,' he insisted. 'If we blatantly conduct campaigns in Fair-Folk territory we could lose all. I know what you are thinking,' he had continued. 'I am attempting to save humankind at the cost of our humanity. But I know not what else to do.' And again, he forbade any human to interfere.

Eventually, Kob stopped arguing. He could see that the decision troubled Tad hugely. It was only as he was leaving that he realized that he was not human. Neither were the Vandals.

So now the Orc and a team of Vandals went out into Fair-Folk territory whenever they could, and they shepherded human refugees to the wall and to freedom.

The latest group was particularly pathetic. A father and two daughters, all malnourished to the point that their faces looked like Halloween masks, skeletal and filthy. Their clothes were little more than ragged strips of sacking and their bodies were covered in open sores.

After Kob and Grim-son, the Vandal Wing Commander, had convinced the humans that they were on their side and they had fed and watered them, the father introduced himself.

'My name is Gareth,' he said. 'These are my daughters, Janet and Phoebe. We escaped from the labor camp in Carlisle. It's a farming and wood cutting encampment. My wife, Sarah, died from some sort of fever a year ago. I was young when the Fair-Folk first arrived and then took over; much later, both my daughters were born. That was just before the rubber heads started the enforced labor system.

We have been incarcerated for almost six years. Allowed out of the pens only to work the fields, no eating utensils, no chance of getting hold of anything that one could make a weapon out of. Under constant Orc guard.

One day, one of the other inmates in our pen died, I hid his body in the straw until the flesh had rotted enough for me to remove his leg. The stench in the pits was already so dire that the Orcs didn't even notice. Once his flesh had decomposed enough, I took off his shin bone and spent the next three weeks sharpening it against the wall whenever I could. Finally, I had this.'

He pulled a six-inch-long shiv from beneath his ragged loin cloth. It had obviously been carved from a human tibia. A vicious weapon.

'One morning, when the Orc opened the pen, I stuck this in his eye. The three of us made a run for it.' He frowned as he spoke. 'The strange thing is, no one else made a break. They just stood there, eyes blank. Like cows waiting for the Judas goat. I don't get it. Anyway, it took us two weeks to get here. I must admit, when we first saw you, we thought that our lives were over.'

'No,' said Kob. 'Your lives have just begun. Well done, you are a brave man, and now you and your family are safe. We shall make the wall by late tomorrow.'

Tears started to flow unbidden down Gareth's face. 'I'm sorry,' he said as he dashed them away with the back of his hand. 'It's just that I have been so scared the past few weeks.'

'There is no need to apologize,' said Kob. 'True bravery is the ability to perform even though you are scared half to death. But now you can relax. Come,' he continued. 'Let us prepare for the journey to your new lives.'

Tad massaged his right knee and grimaced. Arthritis.

'I'm getting old,' he said to himself as he poured a half mug of a concoction that Gogo had made for him. He wasn't exactly sure what it contained but he knew some of the ingredients were ginger, flax seed oils, fish oil, and willow bark. One thing that he did know—it tasted awful. But it did seem to help ease the stiffness and the pain. She had also given him a bottle of pepper oil to rub into the joint, and he did so at least twice a day.

There was a loud knocking on his front door. He cursed, rolled his pants leg down and hobbled to the door, favoring his knee as he did so.

The banging continued without

abating. Not frantic, merely loud, and constant.

'Settle down,' he yelled. 'I'm coming.' He yanked the front door open. 'What?'

'Hell, if I'd known that you'd become such a cantankerous old dude I wouldn't have come back.'

'Nathaniel?'

'The one and only,' said the Marine as he went down on one knee and hugged his friend.

'I knew that you would come back,' said Tad. 'But I must admit I was starting to lose faith.'

'How long has it been?' asked Nathaniel.

'Twelve years and some months,' answered The Little Big Man. 'I'm getting on to sixty years old.'

Nathaniel stood up and looked at his friend. A flash of concern crossed his face, but he hid it quickly with a smile.

However, Tad noticed the fleeting

expression. 'I know,' he said. 'I look like crap.'

Nathaniel didn't deny Tad's observation, he merely shrugged.

'I didn't get any of your postcards,' quipped Tad. 'I assume that you did write?'

'Of course I did,' said Nathaniel. 'Maybe they got lost, even though I made sure to address them to, cantankerous old dude, Earth.'

The Little Big Man laughed, then his face got serious. 'It hasn't been an easy twelve years,' continued Tad. 'The first few were constant battles, defending the new wall. We have had to change the way that we live merely to ensure our survival, all that we do is farm for food and watch the wall. Little time for art and introspection. Our children learn how to survive—not how to live.

We don't have the strength to go on the offensive, and as a result, the rubber heads have subjugated humanity to such an extent that the humans on their side of the wall are treated as little more than dray animals. Mere beasts of burden. Worse than slaves. They are being starved and beaten to death, while we cower behind the wall eking out our survival like craven cowards.' Tad took a deep breath. 'Well, whatever. How are you? Where have you been?'

Before Nathaniel could answer, a young woman of about twenty years old walked into the room. She was small with long, thick auburn hair and hazel eyes. She stood with her hands on her hips and looked at Nathaniel, one eyebrow raised. 'Hey, Dad,' she addressed Tad as she took in the sight of the tall, well built, dark-haired man standing in the doorway. 'Who is this, and why are you making him stand on the threshold instead of inviting him in?'

Tad turned to the woman. 'Oh, Stephanie,' he said. 'This is …'

But Nathaniel shook his head almost imperceptibly before The Little Big Man could say who he was, and Tad had to change his introduction. 'This is … an old friend of mine. He lives over at Land's End. Fishing. Haven't seen him for years.'

Stephanie curtsied. 'Welcome, Dad's friend,' she said with a grin. 'I'm Stephanie. My older sister, Clare, is with friends. Please come in, I shall fix a snack and something to drink. I apologize for my father's manners; he gets confused due to his exceptional old age.'

Both Tad and Nathaniel laughed and followed Stephanie to the sitting room.

When Stephanie had left the room to fix food and drink, Tad turned to Nathaniel. 'Why the secrecy?' he asked.

'I don't want everyone to know that I am back,' answered Nathaniel. 'I have plans, and they require a certain amount of secrecy.'

'Who can I tell?' enquired Tad.

'Aside from you, Kob, Sam, Roo, and Cha-rek. After that we shall see.'

Tad shook his head sadly. 'Roo has gone,' he said.

'How?'

'He got old,' answered Tad. 'He was almost eighty. He just wore out. Went to bed, never woke up. I'm sorry.'

'And the rest?'

'Sam is well, the walking people flourish under his leadership. Cha-rek has handed over the reins of his leadership to Grim-son, the Wing Commander. I made Kob general of our army. He is the same. I give him orders, he ignores them, we muddle along.'

Stephanie came in carrying a tray. On it was an array of smoked meats and cheese and two flagons of apple cider. She placed them on the small table in the center of the sitting area and then she sat on one of the chairs and studied Nathaniel with undisguised curiosity.

The men continued talking, small talk. Weather, crops, how many cattle the humans had. After a while, Tad asked his daughter to go and fetch Kob and send a messenger to find Sam and Grim-son.

She stood up and prepared to leave, putting on her coat and scarf. Before she left, she turned to Nathaniel. 'I know who you are,' she said. 'I mean, I would be stupid not to, after all, you are the most famous person that ever lived. There's like, hundreds of paintings of you, and Dad has told me what you look like about a thousand times. He always said that you would come back,' she continued. 'That's why he wouldn't accept the title of king and he kept your crown and axe on the wall at the meeting hall.'

Tad looked shocked, but Nathaniel simply laughed. 'You're a bright young girl,' he said. 'Do me a favor, don't tell anyone, okay?'

Stephanie nodded. 'Lips are sealed,' she grinned. 'But just one thing—I'm not that young.'

The Forever Man laughed again. 'I was king of the Picts thousands of years ago, my sweet girl,' he said. 'Trust me; everyone is young compared to me.'

'Off you go, now,' said Tad, his expression showing his slight embarrassment at the fact that his daughter was flirting with The Forever Man.

Stephanie left with a flick of her hips as she closed the door.

'Right,' said Tad. 'Now, tell me exactly where you've been, and why.'

So, Nathaniel told the Little Big Man about Fulcrum, his training, and a general précis of the last twelve years.

As he finished, Kob arrived with Stephanie and he had to tell his story again. Stephanie sat and listened, her face filled with wonder. Kob reacted as he always did, with seemingly bored indifference.

Next, Sam and Grim-son arrived. Fortunately, as Tad had already heard the story twice now, he told it on Nathaniel's behalf, only stopping every now and then to enquire about a detail that he had forgotten.

Next, Kob told Nathaniel about the plight of the humans under the control of the rubber heads, repeating stories that he had heard from human refugees that he had saved. He also told Nathaniel about Milly, her role as paramount human and her casual cruelness that she hid under a thin veil of concern and caring.

The Forever Man's face was like stone when he heard what Milly had turned into. 'The last time that we met,' he said. 'I knew that she had lost the plot. I should have done something about it then. Instead, I took the coward's way out and simply left.'

'What else could you have done?' asked Tad. 'You could hardly kill someone that you saved as a little girl and cared for all that time.'

'There are always excuses to be weak,' said Nathaniel. 'And so often they are dressed up as reasons of humanity. The fact remains, if I had killed her then I would have saved much suffering.'

'But at what cost to yourself?' asked Stephanie. 'To your humanity.' The Forever Man turned his gaze onto the young woman, and the power in his dark green eyes crackled across her and seemed to flay her very soul. She shrank back, and for a brief moment, she was almost overcome with a deep primeval terror.

But then the Marine's expression changed, and with it, his eyes lightened in color and he reined the power of his emotions in. 'I cannot afford myself the luxury of thinking about my humanity,' said Nathaniel, his voice a harsh whisper. 'After all, I am barely human. I am The Forever Man. I am Alpha. I am Omega. I am the lever that shall move the world.'

Stephanie said nothing as she struggled to draw breath and steady her shattered nerves. She remembered her father telling her of the authority that The Forever Man exuded. The simple visceral power that emanated from him in waves, unstoppable and undeniable. But this was the first time that she had felt it directed at her, and her reaction was a blend of fear, respect, and pure unadulterated desire.

Tad stood up. 'Right, people. It's late. We all need our rest, particularly me. We shall meet early tomorrow, here over breakfast, and plan our next moves. Remember, the king would prefer his return to remain a secret for now, so no talking.'

Everyone got to their feet, Kob, Sam, and Grim-son shook hands with Nathaniel and left.

Stephanie went to make up a bed in the spare room for Nathaniel, and they all said their goodnights and retired for the evening.

'I need to go into rubber head territory,' said Nathaniel as they all sat around the breakfast table. 'I have learned a lot in the last twelve years, but I need to try out my knowledge in a practical way. Theoretically, I can travel almost instantly along ley lines and between standing stones by manipulation of the pulse light.'

'Hold on,' interrupted Tad. 'What are ley lines?'

'Long story,' answered Nathaniel. 'But basically, they are lines of power that connect the stone circles, standing stones, cathedrals, places like that. You can't see them, but they are there, take my word for it.'

'Fair enough,' conceded Tad. 'Go on.'

'Thanks. I need to do a bit of

travelling, check out where all of the rubber head troops are concentrated, where most of the humans are. I have the inkling of a plan, but I need to firm it up.'

'Right then,' said Tad. 'We'll get ready.'

Nathaniel shook his head. 'I'm going alone.'

'No way,' argued Tad.

'I'll be safer alone,' insisted Nathaniel. 'I'll be undercover so there won't be much danger.'

'It isn't possible,' interjected Kob. 'No humans are allowed to walk free. They are chained and under constant supervision. Even the indoor slaves are shackled so they cannot walk quickly, let alone run. Also, you do not look like a slave; they are thin, sickly, almost dead on their feet.'

'I won't be a slave,' argued Nathaniel. 'I'll be an Orc.'

No one spoke for a few seconds.

Eventually Tad said. 'Huh?'

The Marine laughed. ‘I shall be an Orc.’

‘How?’ asked Kob. ‘And please don’t say make up and some sort of disguise.’

Nathaniel laughed again at the absurdity of Kob’s statement. ‘No disguise,’ he said. ‘I simply do this.’

Lights spun and crackled around the Marine, spinning and coalescing as they became brighter and brighter, and, in front of everyone, the Forever Man’s features slowly morphed into those of a full-grown Orc.

There was a stunned silence apart from Grim-son who fell backwards off his chair in surprise.

‘How the … what … are you?’ stammered Tad. ‘Have you glamoured us?’

The Orc that was Nathaniel shook his head. ‘No,’ he answered in Nathaniel’s voice. ‘Nothing as crude as that. Glamoring doesn’t work if you physically touch the person. If I had glamoured you then you would perceive me to be an Orc, but if you actually prodded me, you would feel soft human skin and flesh. Glamouring is simply a disguise. However, I am not disguised. I am an Orc.'

Kob leaned forward, poked Nathaniel in the chest. And then nodded. 'This is an Orc,' he said.

'How do you do it?' asked Tad.

'You got twelve years spare for me to explain?' quipped Nathaniel.

'Fine,' retorted the Little Big Man. 'I'll just accept it. But can you change back now please?'

And the Orc was gone, replaced with The Forever Man.

'I will go with you,' stated Kob.

'No need,' argued Nathaniel. 'My disguise is enough to stay out of trouble.'

Kob shook his head. 'You look like an Orc, but you do not act like an Orc. You do not know any of the customs, the correct way to conduct yourself. You will come across as … odd.'

'Odd?' queried Nathaniel.

Kob nodded. 'You talk too much. You do not stand still. You are always casting your gaze about, searching, questioning with a look. You fidget. To other Orcs you would seem … simple. Not fully mentally formed. Odd. I shall go with you, to instruct you on how to behave like a fully formed adult as opposed to a callow hatchling.'

'Okay,' agreed Nathaniel. 'Point taken. The two of us need to leave as soon as.'

Kob stood up. 'I am ready.'

'Hold on, friend,' said Nathaniel. 'I need to get some supplies together. I need a sword, can't take my axe, it's too recognizable.'

'Fine,' said Kob. 'Pack, I will wait outside.'

Nathaniel chuckled. 'I'll be a few minutes.'

It didn't take long for Tad and Stephanie to organize Nathaniel a pack and a broadsword.

Stephanie handed the shoulder pack to The Forever Man. 'Dried meat, preserved fruit, some herbs, salt, a piece of waxed cloth, and some furs,' she said.

'My thanks, not so young girl,' said Nathaniel with a wink.

Stephanie blushed. 'Be careful,' she said. 'Stay safe.'

Nathaniel shook hands with Sam and Grim-son as he walked out of the door. Then, once again he hugged Tad. 'I won't be that long,' he said. 'I hope to be back in

a week or so. I want you to ready the army, tell them it's some sort of exercise or something, but make sure that they are ready.'

'I shall,' assured Tad. 'As will I have your crown and your axe waiting.'

And then, without fanfare or acknowledgement from his subjects, The Forever Man set off once more to plan war against the Fair-Folk and their minions.

'If we run into Orcs or goblins I shall call you Nat,' said Kob.

'Why?' asked Nathaniel.

'Because that will be your Orc name. Nat.'

'Aren't any Orcs called Nathaniel?'

Kob shook his head. 'Orc names, three letters only. No more, no less. Kob, Nat, Bak, Gon. Three letters.'

'Why is that?' enquired Nathaniel.

'Because,' answered Kob.

The Marine knew better than to ask for more detail. He knew that Kob was not being obtuse or deliberately imperceptive. The Orc genuinely considered "Because" to be an acceptable answer to a question. He saw no reason to enquire any further of the subject, it simply happened "because." To dwell further on it would be an unnecessary waste of time and energy.

It was refreshing in its simplicity and Nathaniel wished that he could embrace that way of thinking for a while. It would provide a rest from his almost unconscious quest for knowledge, for reason, for the rationale behind both thought and deed. But he was doomed to question everything. And the more that he learned, the more that he questioned.

'Oh well,' he thought to himself. 'We can't all be happy with an explanation that baldly states, "The reason that it happens is because it happens".

The two friends continued running in silence, jogging at a comfortable pace that they could keep up all day with ease. Nathaniel had not changed into an Orc yet. Although it took little power it did make him feel uncomfortable. Like he was wearing an ill-fitted suit.

Nathaniel had told Kob that they needed to get a few miles from the wall and into some secluded spot before he conducted any experiments with travel along the ley lines. He wasn't sure exactly what would happen when he invoked the power, and he didn't want to attract unnecessary attention to himself.

After four hours of running Nathaniel called a stop. 'Here,' he said. He pointed south-east. 'This is a ley line. It stretches from the stone circle at Tomnavarie to the Yeavering Battle Stone outside of Northumberland.'

'I'll take your word for it,' said Kob.

'Good. Now look, you stand over there,' Nathaniel gestured towards a large boulder. 'Stand behind it, I'm not sure how much energy the whole process gives off. I don't want you to get hurt.'

Kob shambled over to the boulder and leant against it. 'I'll be fine,' he said.

Nathaniel shrugged and then stood still and concentrated his mind. He felt for the power, separating it into its component parts, weaving it into the ley line and then pushing it towards his goal destination, the

Yeavering Battle Stone.

He made the connection and then allowed it to take him. It was like jumping into a fast-moving river. A shock of cold, a feeling of speed, a split second of disorientation. Then he was there.

Kob saw very little. A swelling of light, a vibration in the air and a soft crackle. And The Forever Man disappeared.

Nathaniel flashed into existence and quickly checked around to make sure that he was alone. Then he stood and stared at the Battle Stone. It wasn't that impressive to look at. Perhaps six feet high, around four feet long, and three feet wide. A rugged chunk of stone set into the ground. But it had been standing there since 1415, commemorating a battle where some four hundred English soldiers defeated a Scottish army of over four thousand men.

'The poor sods,' whispered Nathaniel to himself as he imagined the battle. The Marine knew that those were the days when the English archer was supreme and there was no viable answer to the longbow. Massed archers were the equivalent of a modern-day machine gun emplacement, and the highlanders would have charged again and again until the archers had totally decimated them. Killing them before they even got close to the English battle line.

The Battle of Agincourt had taken place in the same year, in France, where once again, the English archer had proven his unassailability when a mere four thousand of them destroyed a French army of almost fifty thousand.

'It's all about fire power,' said the Marine to himself as he remembered the destruction of the Annihilators in the battle before the Fair-Folk betrayal.

And then, his experiment successfully concluded, he felt for the place that he had come from, concentrated, and reappeared in front of Kob.

'That was quick,' said the Orc.

Nathaniel nodded. 'Now we've got to try it together. Shouldn't be a problem, same as before, but I'll just feed in a bit more power. Are you ready?'

Kob nodded.

'Okay,' said Nathaniel. 'Stand next to me, put your hand on my shoulder and relax.'

The Orc complied, and Nathaniel pulled in the power, concentrated, and launched them into the flow.

Kob spoke first. 'Well, there's something that you don't see every day.'

Nathaniel cast his gaze around. A barren, rock-strewn landscape painted in purples and grays. Three pale dwarf suns in a line across the sky like a string of fake pearls. The air was rank and smelled of sulfur. No plants and no visible life. 'Oops,' he said. 'Took a wrong turn somewhere.'

'Where are we?' asked Kob.

'No idea,' replied Nathaniel. 'I must have radically overcompensated for the extra weight and used far too much power. Seems to be some sort of alien planet. Might be a different time zone, could even be a different dimension.'

'I thought that you studied this for twelve years,' quipped Kob.

'No,' denied the Marine. 'I studied for twelve years but that was all sorts of stuff. Actual travel I only studied for a few months. Probably should have done more time, but I was getting impatient to get back.'

'After twelve years you suddenly got impatient?'

'Yeah well, it is what it is,' answered Nathaniel. 'Now quiet while I concentrate on getting us back.'

Power surged, time split. The current took them away.

The Battle Stone.

'Impressive,' said Kob as he looked around, confirming to himself that they were in the correct place. 'How many beings do you think that you could shift at once?'

'Not sure,' admitted Nathaniel. 'And I'm not sure that I'd like to risk many more. Who knows where we could all end up?'

'Well, you have tested your capability,' prompted Kob. 'So, what do we do now?'

'Now, we head for more populated areas. I need to see where the humans are being kept imprisoned, where the bulk of the Orcs and rubber heads are, their supplies, weapons, everything.'

'Then I suggest we get as close to London as we can,' suggested Kob. 'Maybe the Robin Hood standing stone outside Peterborough.'

Nathaniel pulled out a hand drawn map and unrolled it. 'Show me.'

Kob pointed at the area where the stone was situated.

'Good,' agreed Nathaniel. 'We'll go there.'

The two stood close together, Kob with his hand on the Marine's shoulder. Nathaniel shifted into an Orc in case there were observers when he arrived, then he worked his magiks and they disappeared.

Nathaniel literally shook with rage.

There were rows and rows of the simple wood and steel cages. Steel bars to the front and roof and sides of slats of raw wood. They provided minimal shelter and little else. Each had a shallow hole in the back corner for the humans' toilet needs, and every cage held between six and eight human beings. The stench was unbelievable. The misery and suffering an almost palpable thing.

Nathaniel started to draw in power, preparing to unleash a holocaust on those keeping the humans prisoner.

Kob put his hand on The Forever Man's shoulder.

'Calm,' he said. 'Now is not the time.'

Nathaniel shuddered with the effort as

he slowly unclenched and let the power flow out.

'Come,' said Kob. 'Follow me. Let us check where the main barracks are and see how many Fair-Folk stay here. Then we will leave. The next time we see these people they will be free.'

Nathaniel nodded. 'Thank you, Kob.'

The two of them walked past the pens to the exterior of the camp. This was one of many situated on the outskirts of London. Like the others that they had now seen, it was loosely based on a military camp structure, although the walls were less defensive and more a simple demarcation of the camp boundaries. A wooden

fence, six feet high and not that sturdy. There was no real chance of any of the humans making a run for it, they were shackled and far too weak to offer any serious resistance.

As they got closer to London, some of the camps were slightly different in that they had a pen section that was separate to the masses. These pens were slightly better. They had fresh straw on the floors and basins of water to wash in. There were also slightly more sophisticated latrine facilities. These were the quarters for the human slaves that actually worked in the Fair-Folk residences. Personal slaves. So obviously they had to be a little cleaner. Dressed better. Less offensive to their alien masters.

Nathaniel made a mental note of the approximate numbers in the labor camp, and then he and Kob walked to a secluded spot, and The Forever Man transported them to their next destination.

Once again, the current of power swept them along, and within seconds, they were standing in the area that Nathaniel had been concentrating on.

Behind them was the River Thames. Unlike pre-pulse times, the river was now almost constantly choked with ice due to the change in weather patterns. To their left, in the distance, stood Tower Bridge. It was rusted and much of it was covered in creepers. Also, it was unusable due to the fact that, when the pulse had struck, the bridge had been raised to let a ship through and it was now jammed in that position until it either rotted away or was destroyed.

'We need to go this way,' said Nathaniel as he walked down the road away from the river.

'What are you looking for?' enquired Kob.

'It's called the London Stone,' answered Nathaniel. 'I know that it is here, close, because that's how I got us here. However, I need to see exactly where it is.'

'Why?'

'It's powerful. Very, very powerful,' said Nathaniel. 'And it's one of London's best kept secrets. Fulcrum told me about it. A prehistoric standing stone, right here in the middle of the city.'

Nathaniel turned right and then stopped, searching for some sort of landmark. 'It's close,' he murmured. Then he pointed. 'There.' He jogged down the street and stopped in front of a ruined building, held together by creepers, no glass left in the windows, perhaps four stories high.

He pulled at the creepers, exposing what looked like a fireplace in the wall, except it was protected by rusted iron bars. Behind was a block of limestone. Two feet high, one and a half wide, and one foot deep.

Kob looked distinctly unimpressed. 'Doesn't look like much,' he said.

'Well it is,' said Nathaniel. 'trust me, I can feel the power emanating from it, and that's good because I have a plan and I needed to check that this stone was as powerful as it was rumored to be.'

'Hey, you two,' called a stranger's voice.

Kob and Nathaniel turned to see an Orc patrol walking down the street towards them. An Orc sergeant and eight soldiers.

'Quick,' said Nathaniel. 'Let's smash them up before they sound the alarm.'

'No,' said Kob. 'Let's be a little more subtle, leave this to me. Greetings, Sergeant,' he continued. 'How can we help?'

'Why aren't you in uniform?'

'We are on leave,' said Kob. 'The Master Sergeant gave us some time off.'

The strange Orc looked at Kob, his face a mask of incomprehension. 'What is, "Time Off"?' he asked.

Kob shook his head. 'Darn' he said to Nathaniel. 'I've been with you guys so long that I forgot, Orcs don't get time off. Ever.'

'So, what now?' asked Nathaniel.

'Plan B.'

'What's plan B?'

'Smash them up before they sound the alarm.'

'That was my plan,' said The Forever Man.

'Whatever.' Kob pulled out his sword, a dry rasp of metal on leather.

But before he could attack, The Forever Man reverted to his human form and leapt past him. There was an explosion of movement and sound as Nathaniel struck blow after blow without pause, one following the other so fast as to sound almost like one continuous drum roll. Within seconds all of the Orcs lay on the floor, limbs at twisted angles, some bleeding, some merely broken.

The Marine had not even bothered to unsheathe his weapon.

Kob looked at the fallen Orcs in disbelief. Finally, he spoke. 'Scary.' He nudged one Orc with his foot. 'Dead,' he muttered. 'All of them.'

'Is that a problem?' asked Nathaniel.

'No,' answered Kob. 'I too would have killed them. But I would have needed a sword to do so. I would not have thought it possible to kill warriors such as these with one's bare hands. As I said before, it is … daunting.' He looked at The Forever Man, his face a little wary, but also full of a new level of respect. 'You are not the same human that I knew twelve years ago.'

Nathaniel shrugged. 'We all change.'

'You have not simply changed,' said

Kob. 'You have totally transformed. You are now, truly, a demigod.' The Orc went down on one knee. 'My lord,' he said. 'I offer you my service, for now and forever.'

Nathaniel knew better than to make light of Kob's offer of fealty. It was something that the Orc had never done anything like this before, and although he already did as Nathaniel commanded, The Forever Man perceived that this was more meaningful than simply swearing to follow his commands.

Nathaniel placed his hand on Kob's head. 'Thank you, brave Kob,' he said. 'I humbly accept your offer and I name you Kob Kingsman. Now stand, my friend.'

The Orc stood.

'Now put your hand on my shoulder,' said Nathaniel. 'I think that it's time we went home.'

Light spun, time crunched, and the torrent of power swept them onwards to their destination.

The Free State army had gathered, and they were encamped behind the Antonine Wall. As were the Vandals. Tad and Kob, and the appointed officers, had already told all of the task that lay ahead, and the army had been split up into groups of fifty each.

Seventeen thousand humans, the majority of them males under the age of eighteen. The rest, females and older men. Five thousand Vandals. Over three hundred groups of fifty.

Humanity's final hope.

Master Marine Sergeant Nathaniel Hogan, King Arnthor of the Picts, sovereign of the Free State, and The Forever Man stood on the wall, his axe on his shoulder. And he spoke, his voice enhanced by the power as it boomed and crackled through the air like a living thing.

'Most of you know me,' he said. 'Although some of you were very young when I left. I am Nathaniel Hogan, The Forever Man, and your king. I have died, and I have returned.

Now, I have spent the last week travelling through the rubber head's realm. Through the lands that were once ours. And I have seen things that would make a grown man weep. Our brothers and sisters, our mothers and fathers, locked up in pens not fit for animals. Living in filth. Starving. Forced into slavery and subservience. Beaten to death for the slightest transgression.

And I have seen the rubber heads, wallowing in luxury. Their slightest whim taken care of by the beaten,

manacled human beings that they have enslaved.

I have seen rich farmlands and game aplenty, natural resources, rivers full of fish, and fields of wheat.

I have seen a land of great bounty. A

cornucopia of delights.

Our land. *Our* farmland. *Our* rivers, and *our* fish, and *our* wheat.

And *our* people.

All controlled by the so-called Fair-Folk. But no longer—for this is the day that we begin to take back our lands. Today we march for liberty. Today we march for humanity.

Today we march for freedom.'

As one the army took up the call.

'Freedom! Freedom! Freedom!'

The gate in the wall was opened and the last human army left the safety of the wall, spreading left and right as they got out into the open.

Nathaniel stood on the wall and watched them leave. It would be at least two days before the next part of his plan could be brought to fruition. Now the army had to simply get themselves into position.

The Forever Man's plan was both straightforward and unbelievably difficult at the same time. The initial part was simple; the groups of fifty had to spread out across the country, stretching from east to west. This would put each group between five hundred and one thousand yards apart, depending on where they were in the country. Basically, a broken front marching across England, each group in line of sight of the next one, but no group large enough to do any serious harm to the massive Orc and goblin army. Above them would fly smaller groups of Vandals, armed with ground attack darts and crossbows.

The group in the center would be larger by four times. Roughly two hundred warriors, and in that group would be Tad and Kob. Nathaniel had insisted that their group be larger to provide them more protection.

And that was when Nathaniel's plan became excessively complex.

Before The Forever Man had put forward the plan to Tad and Kob he had gone into the mountains by himself and had done a small practice run. After a few false starts it had worked admirably. But he now had to replicate the same thing at almost three hundred times the size and scale.

He hoped that he could do it.

And so, the last hope of human freedom marched across the land, heading for London and confrontation with an army that would outnumber them at least sixty-to-one.

Unless The Forever Man could be the lever that would shift the balance. The counterweight on the pulley that would move the world.

He waited until the group in front of him was almost at the horizon, some two and a half miles away, then he concentrated, cleared his mind, and let himself be swept up by the power.

Almost instantly he appeared in front of the distant marching group, surrounded by a shimmer of light. He held up his hand and they stopped their forward march. They had already been told that he would materialize out of nowhere, so although some were obviously spooked, they weren't actually surprised.

'Form up in five rows of ten,' commanded Nathaniel as he walked up to the squad leader.

The squad leader saluted, fist to his chest. 'My king.'

'Thomas,' responded Nathaniel. Then he greeted Tad and Kob with a nod. 'Right, people,' he continued as he addressed the rest of the group. 'Up until now I have kept my plans secret. That is for two reasons, firstly, we do not want the rubber heads getting wind of what we are doing, and secondly, I didn't want everyone to think that I had gone cuckoo.'

There was a ripple of laughter in the squad.

Nathaniel smiled back. 'Before I start, I want you all to know how very proud that I am of you all. I asked you to take to the field and march on an army that outnumbers you by over sixty-to-one and not one of you even hesitated. You truly are men of men and women of women. You are the best of the best, and I thank you.'

As one they responded. 'Hoo-ah!'

'Hoo-ah,' agreed the Marine. 'Now all of you stand still, this requires a certain amount of concentration on my behalf, so no movement and no noise.'

The Forever Man drew in power. He folded the different colors together, melding them into a tangible force. All about him light crackled and spat as his magiks built and expanded.

Then, with a gesture, he released them.

And, standing next to the squad of two hundred human warriors was another similar squad. They cast shadows on the ground, they breathed, they shifted from foot to foot. But when Nathaniel went up to them and touched one, his hand simply passed through the image giving off a small sputter of energy as it did so.

There was a collective gasp from the squad, apart from Tad and Kob who had been forewarned.

Thomas cleared his throat.

'Yes, Thomas,' asked Nathaniel.

'Sorry, my king,' said Thomas. 'But, what are those?'

'They are simulacrums,' answered Nathaniel. 'More than a simple image, but less than the reality. When you move they will move with you. I have imparted enough energy to ensure that they will flatten the grass, leave tracks, and most importantly, make a sound when they walk. But they cannot fight nor help in any way.'

'Begging your pardon, sire,' continued Thomas. 'But what are they for?'

Nathaniel smiled. 'They are part of a ruse, good Thomas. But wait, I have not yet finished.'

The Forever Man concentrated again. And another squad appeared. Then another, and another. Within minutes, the original squad of two hundred human warriors were surrounded by a full two thousand simulacrums. Nathaniel gestured, opening his arms wide and the simulacrums started to march both left and right, spreading their ranks as they did so.

'I shall now do the same with every squad that we have,' he told Thomas. 'So, by the end of today, when the rubber head scouts see us coming they will not see three hundred groups of fifty warriors—they shall see six hundred thousand warriors stretched from coast to coast and advancing upon them ready to do war. The mere sound of their marching feet will be enough to drive the blade of fear into any man's heart, let alone the cowardly hearts of the Fair-Folk leaders. We shall drive them before us like chaff before the wind, forcing them to retreat to the perceived safety of the headquarters in London, and once they are there, they shall feel the full might of The Forever Man.'

Tad led the squad in their battle cry. 'Oorah! Oorah! Oorah!'

Nathaniel pulled in the power and cast himself into the stream, moving onwards to the next squad of human warriors.

For the first time in his long life, Commander Ammon was at a total loss.

'That is impossible,' he said to Seth, the chief mage.

'Impossible or not,' answered Seth. 'It is happening.'

'But where did they all come from?' asked Ammon. 'We know, for a fact, that there are less than twenty thousand human warriors.'

'It appears that our facts have been incorrect,' said Seth.

Ammon shook his head. 'Show me,' he commanded.

Seth nodded, stepped forward and put his hands on either side of his commander's head.

The images sprang into Ammon's mind, allowing him to see and hear the advancing force, as if he was one of the scouts that were looking at it that very moment.

Stretched across the land from left to right, as far as one could see, marched a host of human warriors the like of which Ammon had never seen before.

The air was filled with the rolling thunder of their footsteps and the ground shook under their feet in cadence to the hundreds of thousands of marching feet. The sun reflected off the blades of countless spears, and above them flew thousands of Vandal fighters.

Ammon's heart hammered in his chest like a caged animal as the enormity of the advancing enemy almost overwhelmed him.

'Show Milly,' he commanded Seth. 'I would like her input on this.'

The mage approached the human Milly and he clasped her head, showing her the image of the advancing human host.

Milly went pale as the vista was revealed to her. 'There must be millions of them,' she gasped.

'Approximately six to seven hundred thousand,' corrected Seth.

'But our army still outnumbers them,' pointed out Milly.

'Numerically, yes,' admitted Ammon. 'But the humans are exemplary warriors. Particularly when The Forever Man is in charge.'

'But Nathaniel is dead,' said Milly. 'He hasn't been seen for over a decade. You killed him at the wall after the last battle with the Annihilators.'

'True,' admitted Ammon. 'But the dwarf is also a very adequate tactician.'

'But where did they all come from?' questioned Milly. 'There is something not right here. They couldn't have come from across the sea, there are only a small amount of humans in Ireland, and they tend to keep themselves to themselves. We would have noticed any vast fleets of ice ships coming over from the old Europe.

And anyway,' she continued. 'No sign of other humans has been detected since the pulse.'

'I have a theory,' said Seth.

'Go on,' prompted Ammon.

'What if they are not humans?'

'Well, they patently are,' quipped Milly. 'We have all seen them.'

'Bear with me,' said Seth. 'I am not saying that they are not humanoid. They definitely look like humans. What I am saying is, it might be possible that they have

arrived here in the same way that we did, or the Annihilators or the Vandals. They may look like humans but be alien to this planet. Now, if that is true it is quite possible that, taking their obvious similarities into account, they have bonded with the humans and have entered into some sort of alliance.'

No one spoke for a while as they digested Seth's theory.

'That seems logical,' admitted

Ammon when he finally spoke.

Milly nodded. ‘It’s the only explanation that makes any sense.’

‘So, what do we do?’ asked Seth of his commander.

Ammon thought for a while and then he asked. ‘How many days until they reach us here in London?’

‘I would say, three,’ guessed Seth. ‘At their current pace.’

‘Well, firstly, if we decide to work on the assumption that your theory is correct, then we need to find out if these newcomer human-lookalikes are the same redoubtable warriors that the Earth humans are. If they are, then we shall need to pull back and concentrate all of our strength here, defending London. If, however, they are less formidable than their Earthly peers, we shall revisit the scenario. Agreed?’

Both Seth and Milly nodded their agreement.

‘So,’ continued Ammon. ‘If memory serves me correctly, we have a sizable garrison based in Kettering. Roughly thirty thousand Orcs and ten thousand Goblins. May even be a few trolls. Get word to them, Seth. Tell them to take to the field to attack the enemy line. No retreat. No surrender. We shall gauge the enemy's strength on the outcome of that skirmish and then set the rest of our plans accordingly. How close are the humans to Kettering?'

'They are almost there, Commander,' answered Seth. 'A mere few miles away at most.'

'Good,' said Ammon. 'Send word to them immediately. They must attack at once.'

Exhaustion. There are other words to describe it. Words like weariness, fatigue, and tiredness are but a few. None, however, came anywhere close to describing how The Forever Man felt.

He had been channeling enough life light energy through himself to maintain six hundred thousand simulacrums, giving them body and weight enough to convince the Fair-Folk that they were facing a real flesh and bones army.

He had also had to keep a watch over the entire marching front, ready to react to anything that the Fair-Folk might throw at them. This meant that he had not slept nor eaten for three whole days and nights. And he had not even started on the difficult parts of the exercise yet. That would come later.

Nathaniel scanned through the groups, using the power to skip from one to the next, viewing their situation in a second or two and then moving on.

When he got to the group advancing on Kettering, he stopped and materialized himself next to the leader of the squad. A young woman by the name of Luci.

She flinched in surprise as he appeared, but quickly gathered herself.

'My king,' she greeted. 'We are honored.'

'Don't be,' said Nathaniel. 'I'm only here because you are about to be attacked. There is a force of Orcs and goblins over that hill.' The Marine pointed. 'They are coming this way. Plenty of them. Thirty thousand or so.'

Luci went pale, but to her credit, she did not panic. 'I assume that the simulacrums can't fight, sire?'

Nathaniel shook his head.

'Oh well,' she continued. 'We shall do our best.'

'Don't sweat it, Luci,' said Nathaniel. 'I'm not here to ask you to fight to your death. I'm here to make the enemy fight to his death. But I thank you for your loyalty.' He smiled. 'You are a brave lady.'

Luci looked pleased but still worried. 'I am sorry, sire,' she said. 'But I am not sure that I understand.'

'Tell your men to stand back, Luci,' commanded Nathaniel. 'When the Orc army comes over the hill I am going to unleash hell. The rubber head commanders are obviously testing us, and I want to ensure that they are well convinced that they face a devastatingly superior force, so a lot is going to ride on this, I only hope that I can do it.'

'We have faith in you, sire,' said Luci.

Nathaniel winked at her. 'Thanks.' He walked forward, placing himself a little in front of the line of human warriors and simulacrums. Then he waited.

The Orcs and goblins came over the hill at a fast jog, shields interlocked, and spears held upright.

In typical Fair-Folk military style there was no discernable plan. No flanking maneuvers, no reserves—simply a head-on charge by Orc warriors that were designed and bred for exactly such warfare.

The Forever Man closed his eyes as he concentrated. What he was about to do was the physical equivalent of doing mental calculus whilst reciting *pi* out loud and writing a poem down at the same time.

He had to maintain the presence of the simulacrums across the country, he had to keep an awareness of what was happening all along the advancing human line, and finally, he had to repel an advance of thirty thousand plus troops single-handedly. And all without having slept for three days and nights.

'Child's play,' he whispered to himself as he started to draw in power.

First, he drew in blue, indigo, and violet. Then he built it, laying it out in front of him like an azure highway. Finally, he drew in the hidden dark light, zylac. The cold light of death. He wove them together.

Then he cast his consciousness wide, looking for moisture. Water in snow, in the air, in the trees.

The Orc army came closer and closer, the ground shuddering under their feet as they picked up their pace.

All about Nathaniel a subtle fog rose into the air, climbing above the area like a low-lying cloud.

The Orc army roared its battle cry and broke into a sprint. 'Kamateh!'

Steam poured off The Forever Man as the energy that he was using raised his body temperature to almost boiling point. Waves of pain crashed over him, surging and grinding, as his body died and was reborn second by second.

The Orc army was now close enough to smell. The oiled armor, the leather, the sweat.

And The Forever Man opened his arms wide and roared out his command.

'Ice.'

Immediately, the low cloud coalesced

into hundreds of thousands of baseball sized chunks of solid, blue-white ice.

The charging Orcs leveled their spears in one well-rehearsed movement. 'Kamateh!'

And The Forever Man brought his hand together in front of him. 'Now!'

The ice rocks in the sky above them unleashed themselves in a storm of unbelievable ferocity, smashing down into the ranks of the charging Orc and goblins like shrapnel from a thousand, thousand grenades.

The wounds that they caused were horrific. Sharp shards sliced through leather armor and flesh, laying it open to the bone. Whole chunks smashed bones and skulls, driving the enemy to its knees.

Wave after wave of ice missiles were sent streaking into the enemy ranks, killing and maiming until the ground was over a foot deep in blood-red hail and dismembered limbs and bodies, both dead and almost dead.

And still The Forever Man did not

stop. In fact, he redoubled his efforts and the storm of ice swept through the ranks at an ever-increasing rate, the missiles escalating until the sound of ice striking flesh was a constant drumroll of death and destruction.

The human warriors turned their heads away and Luci started to weep openly at the vista of absolute horror that was unfolding in front of her. For, although all knew that the Orcs and goblins were the enemy and that their destruction was necessary, the onlookers were human, and to be human is to feel emotion.

The devastation continued for almost an hour. Until every living being on the field had been utterly destroyed, beaten and broken, and slashed to death and then buried under a deluge of ice.

Nathaniel had fallen to his knees. His breath rasped in and out like an old bellows. His chest heaving as he desperately tried to take in enough oxygen to keep upright. A tsunami of pain crashed through his body, almost dispossessing him of his senses.

Luci knelt down next to Nathaniel. She put her arm around his shoulders to comfort him but immediately pulled back as the heat coming off him scorched her clothes and blistered her skin.

'Water,' gasped The Forever Man.

She handed him her open canteen and he upended it over his head. Clouds of steam boiled off him. By the time he had poured all of the water out of the container the steam had stopped.

With unsteady legs he climbed to his feet, stood, and took in a few deep breaths. 'Keep advancing, Luci,' he told the squad commander. 'I need to tell Tad and Kob what has happened. Don't worry, I'll be keeping an eye on you. On all of you.'

Luci saluted as The Forever Man shimmered in front of her and then disappeared.

He coalesced next to Tad and Kob a few seconds later.

The Little Big Man jumped sideways, Kob didn't move at all.

‘Hell,’ exclaimed Tad. ‘Can’t you ring a bell, or make a noise before you do that? I almost have a heart attack every time it happens.’

‘Sorry about that,’ said Nathaniel. ‘Listen. I got news. The squad advancing on the area around Kettering was attacked. Forty thousand plus Orcs and goblins.’

Tad went pale. ‘That is not good,’ he said.

‘No worries,’ countered The Forever Man. I took care of it.’

‘How?’

‘Ice storm. Frozen missiles the size of baseballs. Deadly stuff.’

‘You got them to retreat using ice?’ asked Tad, his voice incredulous.

‘No,’ denied Nathaniel. ‘I *destroyed* them using ice. Every last one of them. I had to do something big, go large or go home. It was an obvious test of strength by the rubber head command, and now they are under no illusions that the force they are facing is capable of overwhelming acts of destruction.'

Neither Kob nor Tad said anything for a while, they simply stared at the man next to them. A man who was their friend. A man who had stood with them against all odds for many years now. A man who was now capable of destroying over forty thousand living beings with little more than a thought.

Tad shuddered. Then he looked closer at his friend. And he saw the haggardness of his features. He saw the turmoil behind his eyes. A mélange of horror and despair, and righteousness and duty. And fear. But not fear of the enemy—fear of himself. Fear of what he had become. Of what he was capable of.

And over it all a dull cover of utter exhaustion.

Tad put his hand on Nathaniel's arm. 'You need to rest, my friend,' he said. His voice low and full of compassion. 'A few hours' sleep. If you carry on at this rate it will be the death of you. Or whatever. Something bad will happen, of that I am sure. You've been running on empty for days now.'

Nathaniel shook his head. 'Can't sleep. Need to maintain the simulacrums. We need to get the rubber heads to pull back to London. I need them all there, inside the city, close together so that I can institute the next part of the plan.'

'Forgive me, my king,' said Kob. 'I need to ask, why all of this subterfuge? If you are capable of destroying an army of forty thousand, surely we can simply bide our time and destroy the Fair-Folk piecemeal.'

Nathaniel shook his head. 'Many reasons, Kob Kingsman,' he said. 'Firstly, I cannot begin to tell you how difficult that was. Theoretically I cannot die, but in actuality, if I literally burn up, then there is nothing to stay alive. I doubt that I could do something like that ice storm again and live through it. Secondly, if we start a long, protracted war, who knows what effect it will have on the enslaved humans? Will the rubber heads kill off all of those who are not necessary to the war effort? Will they use them as human shields? Finally, I have enough left in me for one more big hit—and that will be when the rubber heads mass in London. Three more days if all goes well. Just three more days.'

Commander Ammon was close to losing control of his emotions. He had just witnessed the total destruction of an army of forty thousand Orcs in under a single hour. The scale of the power involved was off the scale. It was completely overwhelming, and his brain was struggling to catch up and formulate some sort of response.

'Just bring everyone back,' he shouted at Seth. 'I want the mages circle in the main tower and ready to fight. I want two hundred thousand archers between me and them. Put every Orc that we have around the walls. Dig trenches, raise stakes. Do it!'

'Commander,' interjected Seth. 'If I may make a suggestion? Before we pull everyone back, I think that we …'

‘I am commander, master mage. I am, not you. Do as I have commanded. We have little time; we need to show a united front against these incoming forces. If we can show them enough strength we might give them pause for thought.’

Seth bowed and left the room. As he closed the door he saw Milly approaching, walking down the corridor. He grabbed her wrists.

‘Milly human,’ he said. ‘You must talk to the commander. We need to discuss what to do. I believe that he is wrong in telling us to pull back to London. There must be other alternatives.’

Milly stared at the mage, her gaze icy. ‘Don’t you think that you could best serve your commander by simply obeying him?’ she asked.

‘There is something not right,’ insisted Seth. ‘I can’t put my finger on it, but I genuinely believe that we would gain nothing by overreacting so quickly, after all, a day won’t make a difference.’

‘I tell you what,’ answered Milly. ‘I

will do you a favor.'

Seth bowed. 'Thank you, Milly human,' he said.

'Yes,' continued Milly. 'When I go in to see the commander, I will forget that this conversation occurred. After all, now is not the time for Commander Ammon to discover that his closest advisor is attempting to undermine his authority.'

Milly turned on her heel and entered the commander's room without announcing herself. She closed the door firmly behind her.

Seth shook his head and left in order to carry out his commander's orders.

Nathaniel had been riding a horse but had now taken to walking in order to keep himself from passing out from exhaustion. He stumbled slightly as he walked, his legs loose and rubbery. It was the morning of the fifth day, and as the humans advanced, they started to come across abandoned labor camps and small settlements. The human slaves were still in their pens but there was no sign of Orc nor goblin nor Fair-Folk.

Nathaniel had given instructions that, whenever any squad came across human prisoners the squad leader would allocate a certain number of the squad to stay with them, find them food and generally do all that they could to help. Nathaniel had said that more would be done for them when the final battle was over.

The Marine stumbled again and Kob grasped his arm to steady him.

'It's working,' said Tad. 'The rubber heads have pulled back to London. Not sure how that helps,' he continued. 'You can't keep up this ruse for much longer, and the moment they see that it's all smoke and mirrors we are going to have a million unhappy Orcs and goblins itching for a fight.'

'It won't get to that,' said Nathaniel. 'I hope,' he added.

'You hope?' said Tad. 'Oh, great. That fills me with confidence.'

Nathaniel raised an eyebrow. 'Have faith.'

Tad smiled. 'I do, my friend,' he said. 'I really do. So then, what now?'

'Now,' answered The Forever Man. 'I put a finish to this.'

'How?' asked The Little Big Man.

'I need to get to London. The London Stone, to be exact. Once I am there, then I need a few moments to set the rest of my plan in motion.'

'When?' asked Kob.

'No time like the present,' responded Nathaniel. 'The sooner the better and all that.'

'I will come with you,' volunteered Kob. 'You will need help.'

Nathaniel nodded. 'Thank you.'

'I will also come,' said Tad.

Nathaniel shook his head. 'No,' he said. 'The people need a king.'

'Good,' said Tad. 'Because they have one—you.'

'No. When you get back to the Free State, you must take the crown. You must be king.'

'Why me?' asked Tad. 'Why not you?'

Nathaniel went down on one knee and put his arms around his friend. Neither of them spoke. There was too much to say, and there was nothing that could be said.

Then The Forever Man stood up and

nodded at Kob. 'Let's go.'

The Orc put his hand on Nathaniel's shoulder.

Color raged, and time twisted, and they were gone.

And the tears rolled unheeded down The Little Big Man's cheeks as he stood alone.

***

Nathaniel and Kob materialized at the top of the street that housed the London Stone.

Unfortunately, unlike the last time they had materialized there, the street was full of Orcs and Nathaniel had simply not had enough spare energy to disguise himself.

The Marine unclipped his axe and Kob drew his broadsword, then without pause, they simply attacked, driving their way through the packed Orcs towards the London Stone that was halfway down the crowded street.

It took a few moments for the startled

Orcs to respond, and by then, at least ten were down. But there were still many to go, and they quickly rallied, drawing their weapons, and charging at The Forever Man and his friend.

Kob fought like a being possessed, his sword cleaving through the ranks of the enemy like the very scythe of Death himself.

Nathaniel slipped and fell to one knee as waves of fatigue and weariness threatened to overcome him. Five days and nights without sleep, combined with the unbelievable amounts of energy that he had expended, were taking its toll on him, and he was now so exhausted that both his mind and his body were running on empty.

Kob hauled him up by his collar and pushed him forward, and it was with surprise that Nathaniel saw that he was in front of the London Stone.

He swung his axe at the bars that protected the stone, smashing through them as he did so. Then, with a mighty heave, he pulled the steel free and stood next to the stone.

Behind him he could hear Kob redoubling his efforts to keep the attacking Orcs back. To give Nathaniel time.

The Forever Man put his hands on the stone and concentrated, drawing in power. Above him lightning flashed across the sky and massive peals of thunder hammered the land. A vast wind picked up and screamed through the streets of London like a banshee calling for the souls of the damned. All about him windows shattered, and doors blew off their hinges. The ground shuddered as if it were in the throes of death.

Nathaniel could hear the clashes of swords and the scream of the dying all around him as Kob gave his all to protect him for as long as possible. But they were as sounds and happenings from another place. Another world.

The London Stone started to shimmer as it turned from dull gray-brown to a deep orange and then to a fiery red as it heated up, filling with power.

The Forever Man's hands started to blacken and burn, the pain as intense as anything that he had ever felt before. But he dared not let go. He dared not break contact.

He pulled in more power and then, with the skill born of twelve years of training, he started to weave the layers of light together, forming a net of vast size that he spread over the entire city around him.

His clothes burst into flame and he could feel his armor start to melt as the power mounted. The pain was too intense to voice. There was no room to scream, there was no room for anything bar the power and the pain.

Behind him he sensed Kob go down, a blade through his torso. But he rose again and continued to fight, bleeding from over twenty deep cuts, his life pouring from him as he fought on.

The net of light anchored itself to the ground and then started to tighten, pulling itself in, capturing all in its crackling bonds.

White hot needles of agony pierced The Forever Man's very soul as the power mounted to an apocalyptic level, pouring into the London Stone in a waterfall of sound and light. Buildings all around The Forever Man started to explode, masonry and concrete and steel fountaining up into the sky as the ground shook and rumbled and tore apart.

Another spear took Kob in the chest. He heaved himself forward and struck his enemy down with a mighty overhand blow, but the spear remained anchored in his chest, slicing deep into his lungs. He coughed up blood and swung again, dispatching another Orc.

Yet another blade struck him, and then another spear. He fell to his knees. An axe shattered his helmet. Blows rained down on him as he struggled to stand. If he could not delay them any longer then Nathaniel would not have enough time to finish his task.

Kob shook his head, shaking it from

side to side like a wounded bull elephant. And he heard the singing of the human warriors as they stood with him on the wall. He saw Tad's smile as he clasped his hand and called him friend.

He remembered The Forever Man giving him a name.

With a last mighty effort, he stood and roared. 'I am Kob Kingsman!'

And he charged into the fray once again, buying Nathaniel the precious extra seconds that he needed.

Nathaniel sensed his friend go down and he knew that he was out of time. So, he stopped attempting to push aside the pain. Instead, he accepted it. He welcomed it. He used it, adding it to the net of power. Augmenting it with his own suffering. Giving his very life to its existence. He opened his soul and let the London Stone take it to do with it as it willed.

Time stopped.

The sky went dark.

The London Stone shattered into a

million pieces.

And the world moved.

Commander Ammon of the Fair-Folk opened his eyes. At first, they could not focus. All about him was dark. Gray. He looked up at the sky. It was a dead blue color. There was no hint of the life light.

He glanced from left to right. And what he saw filled him with utter dread and despair.

On the right he saw the valley of Southee. And on each side of the Vale, rose the Sethanon Mountains.

He heard a wail of anguish behind him and he turned to see Seth Hil-nu, his chief mage. Next to him stood Milly human, her face a mask of terror.

And spread out beyond them the rest of the Fair-Folk and their minions. The Orcs, the goblins, and the trolls.

‘How is this possible?’ whispered Ammon.

‘Where are we?’ shrieked Milly, the only human there.

‘We are home,’ croaked Seth. ‘We have been sent back to where we came from. Back to our land of origin. Back to darkness. We have been sent back to Death.’ He turned to Ammon. ‘You egotistical fool,’ he said. ‘You’ve destroyed us all.’

And millions upon millions of dark elves came pouring into the valley and over the mountains, and they fell upon the Fair-Folk in an avalanche of destruction.

There is no tunnel.

There is no light.

There is only the unbearable lightness of being. Because the universe and all in it has already occurred and will continue to occur, again and again. *Ad infinitum.*

A leaf in an ocean of eternity.

A single soul lost in an endless moment in time.

Perpetually, eternally, and always.

Unless someone has enough power to stop it. To continue onwards. To prevent us making the same mistakes over and over. A lever to move the world.

A man alone.

Living forever.

The Forever Man.

A tsunami of pain. A bright light. Voices.

Nathaniel opened his eyes.

Above him the pulse light coruscated across the sky. He rolled over onto his front and then slowly levered himself to his knees, fighting the bolts of pain that flashed through him as he moved.

He glanced down at his body. He was almost naked, what remained of his charred clothing hung off him like strips of burned offerings.

Raggedy man.

A large war axe lay on the snow next to him. He picked it up and used it to pull himself to his feet.

Then he looked around. Standing a few yards away were a group of ten men.

One stood next to a horse and the rest were mounted. They were all dressed in a similar fashion. Ten-gallon hats, leather trousers, denim shirts, boots. On their hips, belts with holsters. The holsters looked to contain some manner of old-fashioned, long barreled revolver. They also carried swords and spears.

The man who had dismounted spoke first. ‘Well, goldarnit. Just where in tarnation did you come from, stranger? One minute you wasn’t there and the next you was.’

Nathaniel shook his head. ‘I don’t know.’

‘Well, what’s your name boy?’

Again, the Marine shook his head and shrugged.

‘You simple, boy?’ Continued the man.

‘I don’t think so,’ answered Nathaniel. ‘Where am I?’

The group of men laughed. ‘Well you be in the Unified States of New America.

The good ole USNA. Where else, boy?'

Nathaniel wrinkled his forehead as he thought. He remembered a pulse. A land. A battle? But it was faded. Out of focus and disjointed.

'The pulse,' he said. 'I think that I remember the pulse.'

'What you talking about?' asked the man. 'What's a pulse?'

Nathaniel pointed at the sky. 'Those colors. The light.'

'Oh,' acknowledged the man. 'The High-Light. What about it?'

'Not sure,' mumbled the Marine. 'I think that I remember it happening.'

'I surely doubt it,' laughed the man.

'Why?' asked Nathaniel.

'Because the High-Light appeared over six hundred years ago,' said the man. 'So, unless you be real old, you be mistaken.'

And a voice in Nathaniel's mind spoke to him. But he ignored it because the words made no sense.

The voice said—

'You are The Forever Man … and you have moved the world.'

Hi guys – Well, I hope that you enjoyed this. I know that it was a bit darker than the other installments but, as Tad often says, 'Sometimes life just sucks.' If you did enjoy it, PLEASE could you leave a review? I would really appreciate it. And, once again, if you want to get hold of me please feel free to write zuffs@sky.com It's my personal email and I will get back to you.

Next up – Book 6

REBIRTH.

Please give it a go.

The Forever Man – Book 6

https://amzn.com/B01DJLYEMG

Acknowledgements

Polly—thanks for all the hours of editing & valuable input.

Axel—for the readings and the advice.

Mom & Dad & Shirl—for helping me to remember.

Michael Marshal Smith—my mentor and friend, for telling me to keep writing.

Thanks again for all and speak again soon

Your friend – Craig

Printed in Great Britain
by Amazon